The Grandfather's Mystery

Also by Chandrashekar Nagawaram

Case No. 56

Amita – What if she was here.!

The Grandfather's Mystery

CHANDRASHEKAR NAGAWARAM

PRABHAT
PRAKASHAN

Published by
PRABHAT PRAKASHAN PVT. LTD.
4/19 Asaf Ali Road,
New Delhi-110 002 (INDIA)
e-mail: prabhatbooks@gmail.com

ISBN 978-93-5562-335-5

THE GRANDFATHER'S MYSTERY
by Chandrashekar Nagawaram

Edition
First, 2024

Price
₹ 400 (Rupees Four Hundred Only)

Printed at
SS Japan Art, Delhi

Dedicated to Amma and Baba
and
The people around me who inspire the world

Prologue

I am Aryakt. I am mentally normal, but the world doesn't think so. I am twenty-six now, and I have an engineering degree. I don't work in any multi-national company. Having graduated in Engineering, the world expects me to work in an organisation with at least a five-digit salary. I am a tuition teacher for some school kids. I do not even count the money I get from them. But I know it's good enough for my survival. Those kids are my strength. The world, at times, laughs at me. When I say 'world', I mean 'my world', which is small and contended. I am not aware of what anyone outside my world thinks about me. But my gut says that they'll laugh at me, too.

Education isn't just an allowance to earn money. It brings a sense of awareness—a way of life. Yes, these are my justifications to those who laugh at me for my job and social behaviour. I don't think they are wrong. They want me to grow and build a life inclusive to the world. And the whole problem lies there. They take the literal meaning of the 'world.' And I contain it with a few people and some books.

I don't talk to my house owner while I pay the rent. I don't speak to the milkman while I take the milk from him. I don't talk to the vegetable vendor as I buy them. I am happy living this way. But 'my world' isn't. They want me to speak to everyone. I ask them, why is it so? I am happy living like this.

They say I am living a plain life. The motivation they get roaming around seems to have gotten over their mind, and they feel it's a blessing to socialise. But now, I defer their thought. The motivation that a Monte-Carlo analysis gives me is equally impactful to my life. However, the impact would motivate me to think about another mathematical concept.

Yes, socialising is a good thing to do. But it's not a mandate. One can have rules to limit one's behaviour and voice in front of the world. Imposing a rule to raise the voice is harsh, at least for the people like me. Yes, I am an introvert. I am an extreme introvert. Yes, I have social anxiety. No, I have severe social anxiety.

I feel anxious when 'my world' forces me to align with the world. I feel panic. I feel stressed. When the stress overshadows my thinking ability, I even hallucinate. I speak more to myself than to others. Thank God for giving me the ability to control my panic and stress by reading books. Yes, I read a lot of books. Primarily technical and motivational. And yes, I believe in God.

I think a lot, but I want to keep it to myself. I can talk a lot but speak to only a few people. Only two, in fact. Thanks to Madhava and Sameer. My childhood friends. Big part of 'my world.'

My students complete my world. I am never in a panic while talking to kids. They are transparent in their thoughts. They speak what they think. That makes me connect with them. Some students are over twelve, but I still call them kids. They will always be kids for me. I enjoy being with them, and with what they say, they also enjoy being with me. Education shouldn't be kept undistributed.

At the age of twenty-six, I should wish for lovely parents, a great job earning big money, a beautiful and caring girlfriend, many friends, great career aspirations, and a blissful retirement.

But I never wished for at least one of these. I am just happy with what I am doing now. But frankly, I miss the feeling of having parents.

My heart floats everywhere when I think about my parents. I don't know about them at all. They were dead, for what I know. The orphanage where I grew up doesn't know them. The orphanage knows my grandfather, who admitted me to it. He cannot talk as his brain nerves seem to be taking rest for many years. I beg your pardon – it's my way of explaining things. He is in a coma.

Coming back to parents, Mother – how it would be to be with her. I wonder how it would be to sleep in her lap, as many writers use the phrase. Does she make such a difference in life? How powerful the world portrays her very existence. It's almost divine. But for me, she remains a mystery for the hype surrounding her power. However, I can feel the aura of her existence. And yes, I wish I had lived with her at least for a day. I want to see how it could affect my thoughts. I might not have spent any time with her, but I can connect to her aura that the world portrays.

Father – definitely whose rigour and achievements are discounted, for what I know from 'my world.' I don't know if 'Father' could create an aura similar to a mother, but I feel he deserves much more than what the world gives him. As his reputation goes, my mind thinks about him, but 'Mother' occupies most of it. I can connect to the writers as they say, "Father is the one who is there for you when the mother can't provide something." So, the father has to wait for his turn. Truly harsh.

I think about them, and at times, I miss their presence. 'My world' would have been the same had it been the same instances around me. Time doesn't hold itself in its world like I do. It has its ways to bring peace and storm whenever it wants and as needed.

It was all peace for me so far. Now, as this storm arrives in my contained life, I feel broken, confused, and in panic, but more importantly, I feel afraid.

I had never guessed that my grandfather, who had been in a coma for the past twenty-two years, held a big secret in him. As it gets revealed unusually, I fear it'll break me apart altogether. I wish I could have myself together.

But.....

❑

Acknowledgements

Maatru devo bhava.!
Pitru devo bhava.!
Acharya devo bhava.!

My heartful thanks to my family – Swapna, my wife. Kaushik and Kashvi, our twins. No effort is meaningful without your support and encouragement. A special note of thanks to my daughter Kashvi and son Kaushik for suggesting the book title.

Thanks to Sudheep Sudhakaran for being a courteous critic of my work and being available all the time.

Thanks to Ramya Sahithi Jayanthi for being my proofreader and patiently handling my 'take her for granted' mindset.

I am thankful to Sesidhar DVSR for inspiring me by example.

Thanks to Alok, Pradeep Raj, Vijay Kumar, and Hari Prasad for their crucial input in developing this story.

Thanks to all my well-wishers for keeping me motivated all the time.

Music activates my nerves and evokes me to create stories. I am hugely thankful to all those music composers whose tunes have triggered me to create this story.

The purpose is fulfilled when the thoughts are shared. With due respect, I thank all my readers for spending their time reading this novel. We are always connected with our thoughts.

❑

Contents

Prologue 7

Acknowledgements 11

Chapter 1 15

Chapter 2 19

Chapter 3 28

Chapter 4 38

Chapter 5 46

Chapter 6 54

Chapter 7 59

Chapter 8 62

Chapter 9 66

Chapter 10 73

Chapter 11 78

Chapter 12 82

Chapter 13 87

Chapter 14 91

Chapter 15 96

Chapter 16 100
Chapter 17 104
Chapter 18 108
Chapter 19 115
Chapter 20 119
Chapter 21 125
Chapter 22 133
Chapter 23 139
Chapter 24 146
Chapter 25 152
Chapter 26 158
Chapter 27 165
Chapter 28 175
Chapter 29 183
Chapter 30 189
Chapter 31 196
Chapter 32 201
Chapter 33 208
Chapter 34 221
Chapter 35 229
Chapter 36 238

Chapter 1

As the early morning rays pierced through the thin voile fabric of the window curtain, Madhava stood leaning on the writing table near the whiteboard. Folding his arms tight, he looked at the kids seated on the floor mat. They immersed themselves in their books.

Madhava looked at Sameer, who enveloped the circumference of the metal window with his fingers on the other side of the room. He whistled in a low pitch. Sameer looked at him, but the kids didn't. He, with a bit of surprise, tapped the wooden table. Kids ignored it.

Sameer raised his eyes in surprise. Madhava made some sounds, cleared his throat, and observed the kids. No kid looked at him. As a bit of irritation superimposed his surprise, Madhava spoke.

"Hello everyone!"

Kids looked at him at once.

"Hello, sir!" the kids said in unison.

"Wow!" exclaimed Sameer.

Looking at the kids of various ages behaving similarly, Madhava felt amused. He wanted to ask their names but preferred to make the kids feel comfortable with him and Sameer. Hence, he asked.

"Do you know where your teacher is right now?"

"Nope!" said the seven-year-old Arjun.

"He is seated there, on the chair on the footpath," said Sameer, walking towards the terrace's railing and indicating the kids to join him.

"Fine. We know that chair. Sir prefers that one," said the nine-year-old Govind.

Madhava and Sameer exchanged a glance.

Considering the situation of the day and the previous night, Madhava asked the group a question.

"Well, okay. Let me ask you all a question. What do you think is the best thing in your tuition teacher?"

The kids thought briefly, and then Arjun said, "His walking style."

Before the two friends could take in the unexpected answer, the twelve-year-old Sahasra said, "His eyes, probably!"

"His smile," Govind jumped in.

Madhava looked at them in astonishment. He thought for a moment and said:

"That is very unusual. Don't you think that your teacher should have *teaching* as the best quality? If you do think so."

Eldest of all, the fourteen-year-old Mugdha said at once, "You have asked about the best quality, not 'the perfect' one. He is *perfect* in teaching. 'Best' has its comparison to become 'the best,' but 'perfect' is always 'perfect,' you know."

Madhava looked at her keenly. She meant what she said. Her voice had a gist of pride, even though she was pretty soft with her words.

He then asked, "What about his dressing sense then?"

"It's simple, mostly," she said and then continued after a moment, "Always."

Madhava replied, "I know what you mean. We bought him a nice hoody, cargo jeans and sports shoes. And you know what! He is wearing it now."

Everyone stood up at once and looked at Madhava. Sameer moved beside Madhava, looking at the alertness of the kids.

Sameer added, "Yes. We were at a party last night. And we thought, you know, the new dress will look good on him."

Arjun and Govind ran across and hugged Sameer and Madhava. Sahasra and Mugdha held Madhava's hand. Everyone smiled so gracefully that their smile dominated the brightness of the sun rays that illuminated the penthouse.

"Thank you. Are you both his friends? He used to mention Madhava and Sameer," asked Mugdha.

"Yes, we are. I am Sameer and he is Madhava," indicated Sameer.

"We tried to get him some brand-new trendy clothes many times. He never accepted them. He always wears that simple cotton shirt and shaded jeans. Thank you for getting the clothes for him," said Mugdha, smiling.

"Trendy clothes!" corrected Sahasra.

Everyone laughed and moved to the railing.

The group stood across the railing in a queue. They beamed at the chair on the footpath.

Aryakt was seated on it with his head down. Looking at him, they assumed that his eyes should have been wet. The kids looked at him for some time. He seemed to be bringing himself into this world slowly.

Mugdha looked at Madhava and Sameer and said, "The only blood relative he has is his grandfather, who is in hospital always. He is lonely in his life," she stayed silent for a couple of moments and asked in a changed pitch of voice. "Do you know another 'the best' thing in him?"

"What?" both friends asked at once.

"Wait," she said and looked around.

After around a minute, the sea breeze of Vishakhapatnam overlapped the surroundings. Aryakt moved his head up to set his hair right at once, looking against the direction of the breeze.

Mugdha then arched her right eyebrow and glanced at the two friends, indicating towards Aryakt. As they looked at him, she said:

"His hairstyle. Don't you think so?"

Madhava acknowledged with a smile, and Sameer raised his eyebrows and nodded in agreement.

"He is looking like a hero." said the eight-year-old Vilohith.

"Did the three of you go to a party yesterday? How did you persuade him to attend a party? It is quite unlikely. Rather impossible."

Sameer responded. He said, "Unlikely, yes. But we managed to do so. But..... it was......"

Madhava and Sameer stood silent.

Mugdha then asked in a shallow voice. She seemed concerned about something that made all the kids gather around her.

"What happened?"

Madhava took a heavy sigh and said, "What happened? You should rather ask *what didn't happen.* Everything that probably was unexpected, had happened."

Sameer looked at the kids and nodded.

The kids glared at Sameer and Madhava in silence. ❑

Chapter 2

The Previous Day

As the mobile rang, Sameer felt irritated with its ring. He looked at the clock with half-opened eyes, and the time ticked 7.00 AM. It was Sunday. The firmware release of his latest project was awaited on Monday. He needed sound sleep, and thus, he promised himself to sleep till 10 AM.

As he looked at the mobile screen, his irritated face changed to a surprise. He arched his eyebrows, realising Madhava was on the other side. Sameer knew that Madhava was busy these days with his new startup company. Sameer had already confirmed that he would join Madhava's firm when it was established well (although the defining factor for 'established' was unconvincingly agreed upon by both friends). Sameer knew that his safe play measures throughout his life had aided him in making suitable decisions. Madhava, on the other hand, was an *adventure-boy* always. He took risks, even as a student. After his post-graduation, he joined a multi-national company, and very soon, his designation ramped up to the people manager.

Madhava always rightly believed that he could do a lot more than what he was doing at any point in time. That quality of his has led him to take risks, which proved quite fruitful for him most of the time. Although leading a successful life in the MNC, he changed the company as a vice president of the technology business in a relatively more minor firm. After acquiring tremendous appreciation and increasing the business statistics almost fourfold, his thoughts of setting up his own company have overcome the glory he enjoyed as an employee.

He then quit and started his firm in his favourite technology business. He knew what solutions the world needed. He knew what products the consumers liked. He knew what work Engineers loved. He also learned how to hire and retain employees.

Sameer was a safe player throughout his career. His coding skills have always dominated the skills of other employees - his rating every year was proof of it. He, however, wasn't an adventurer. He believed in his engineering education more than the leadership ideology the world seeks. He thinks other people are looking into it. When Madhava approached Sameer for an offer in his startup, Sameer softly declined it because of his very nature. Madhava anticipated it but had promised Sameer to take him in his company whenever Sameer felt it to be safe getting into it.

The third friend was Aryakt, a calm-going and brilliant person. The three friends studied in Vizag (short form for Vishakhapatnam) until the ninth grade. Aryakt was younger than the other two. For the tenth grade, the families of Sameer and Madhava had moved away from Vizag for personal reasons. Sameer moved to Mumbai, and Madhava moved to Pune. Because of their proximity, they occasionally meet each other's family, but they last met Aryakt long ago.

Aryakt, from his childhood, was very bright in his academics. His technical excellency was radiant. In contrast, he lagged in his social confidence. His reserved nature wasn't a hindrance to his improving excellence, and his only friends - Sameer and Madhava, never realised that that very behaviour would get him into social anxiety. Aryakt was way intelligent for his age. He coached his friends and built confidence in them for their academics. But in this due course, the friends, at that age, couldn't realise that Aryakt, with his social anxiety, was getting himself farther from where he was supposed to be.

Aryakt had lost his parents when he was two (none to validate, but the orphanage records say so), and he didn't have any siblings. None of the paternal or maternal relatives visited him at the time. He does not know where they stay. He does not even remember their faces or names. No one can validate even their existence. The only blood relative he has is his grandfather, Mr. Srivatsa, who has been in a coma for the last twenty-odd years and is taken care of by a trust hospital in Vizag. Aryakt didn't talk to his grandfather anytime but saw him once every three months. He virtually holds a strong bond with his grandfather, and he always wondered what the warmth of the family would feel like.

Around six months back, Madhava shifted to Vizag to set up his startup company. Around two months back, Sameer came to Vizag to sort his property-related things. Both tried to contact Aryakt through social media. Aryakt, not being on any social media platform wasn't a surprise for them. The only hope was the orphanage where Aryakt spent his childhood. They contacted the orphanage, and then they got Aryakt's address. They met their childhood friend after around twelve years. The reunion was both heartwarming and sobering as they confronted some harsh realities. Madhava and Sameer were pretty happy seeing their beloved friend. But Aryakt's problem had broken their heart.

Aryakt had the problem of extreme social anxiety, and his introverted nature added to it. They couldn't believe that Aryakt's reserved nature had only amplified to such a level that his whole lifestyle seemed to be under concern. He lived a mediocre life without any social network. The financial crisis had added to the misery. He didn't have any friends. Neither could he mingle in any group. He always lived alone; the stumbling block was that he was comfortable alone. Psychologically, the need to be social had no significance for him.

Aryakt was highly reluctant to make any changes in his life. The only bothering thing for him was his financial state. However, he never took any loan from anyone, fearing not being able to pay it back. The primary fear was to face the person while asking for the loan. Aryakt did not answer the teacher's questions in school, fearing the attention of his fellow students and the teacher.

This nature of Aryakt exploded on Madhava and Sameer. They never expected the seed of shyness to shape into a monster. They were concerned about him and his future. They couldn't take in that an intelligent, well-behaved, good-looking, and a kind person was getting into an unfortunate situation. Though social anxiety isn't new to the world, the extent to which it had its roots dug in Aryakt's mind was frightening. Having no family or relatives around made the situation pathetic.

They googled about the issue of social anxiety and discovered that it's not a disease but a state of mind. It can be cured through proper medication and therapy. Aryakt never tried to get himself treated for it. And it's been so long that he carries it in, gets quite comfortable with his life, and doesn't fear losing his social life.

The friends tried to get him treated for his problem. They had taken him to a few psychiatrists, but that didn't help much since Aryakt reluctantly visited those doctors. He didn't find it necessary to treat himself. He couldn't even withstand that his friends paid the doctor fees and ultimately refused the doctor visits.

Aryakt never complained about his problems and his life. Madhava and Sameer wanted him to understand that the world is beautiful and that he deserves people around him. He deserves better challenges, a better atmosphere, and a better life.

Madhava had a plan to trigger that initial change.

Setting right himself on the bed, Sameer took Madhava's call.

"Hello, Sameer! I am planning to invite Aryakt to today's engagement ceremony of Anu. It'll be a big party, and everyone will have to participate in some activities. Did you understand where I am trying to get to?"

Sameer took a moment to take in what Madhava said. He thoughtfully replied, "Yes. I get it. But do you think Aryakt can take this?"

"Of course, he can't. But he must get out of the mess he has put himself in. And I do not see any other way out. We'll have to push the fish into the pond for it to understand that it *can* swim."

Sameer gave a weighty pause. He then said, "Right. I can't believe he never attended a function in his life. But do you see him creating any mess in the party?"

"Come on, Sameer. I don't think so. And we'll be with him anyway. Let us get him involved in some activities. And you know, there'll be girls. Many of them." he laughed.

Sameer laughed in response.

"We'll have to get him a nice dress first. And then convince him to come to the party. Let him be prepared for what he'll go through during the evening," said Madhava.

"Okay. When should we be at Aryakt's home for the convincing session?" asked Sameer.

"Before lunch. Let us have lunch with him. And sorry to have woken you up so early on a Sunday. You Techies want to sleep late on Sundays. Don't you?"

"That is alright. A CEO can do whatever he wants with his current, past, or future employees," Sameer replied heartfully.

"See you at Seetamma dhaara. Sharp noon," Madhava replied, laughing.

Aryakt's home was a single-room penthouse with a big open terrace in front of it. He had filled the circumference of the terrace with various plants of rose, lily, jasmine, and other flowers. The terrace looked marvellous and reflected the finesse of isolated beauty in Aryakt's way of life.

The three friends seated on the chairs on the terrace during a cloudy noon spoke to each other without any hesitation. Convincing Aryakt was a complex task on their hands. After an hour of discussion, Aryakt still needed convincing. As he realised the building intensity of his friends to convince him to attend the party, his body started sweating with tension.

"It's not a war you are asked to fight, Aryakt." Sameer sounded irritant.

"For me, it's more than a war. In war, you *will* have a chance to win. But *this* war is already lost for me. The humiliation is an additional punishment." Aryakt replied.

"Why do you want to presume everything? Don't you think it's just a relaxing stuff - a party? Just be there seated somewhere, looking around. No one will disturb you. We'll make sure of it." said Madhava and continued.

"You must come out of this state of mind, Aryakt. And occasions like these are useful for opening up, not by words but by thoughts. You need not speak to anyone. Just observe the happenings. I am sure you'll enjoy it. And one more thing."

Madhava stopped abruptly, and Aryakt gave him an intense look, anticipating additional soldiers joining the enemy's army in this war.

Madhava couldn't stop his laughter from looking at Aryakt's fearful expression. He then said, "Don't panic. I wanted to say that there will be girls. You can try talking to one of them. To break the ice of your rock-solid thoughts."

"Correction - Damped thoughts," said Sameer and continued, "You should take these elderly thoughts from us. How much, Maddy, how young is Aryakt to us?"

"Three years, I guess," Madhava replied.

"That's more than enough for imposing compulsory advice," Sameer said with authority.

"No. Please don't say it is compulsory. It's another war for him. But don't you think Aryakt tried to talk to a girl in school? What was her name? Bindu or something?" Madhava added.

"Let's make it, *Chandu*. Because the gender effect in the name will relax the enemy's artillery in the war, he is fighting." Sameer started laughing and got up from the chair.

Aryakt held his hand with force and pulled him. Sameer got rid of Aryakt and started running. The curtains flew, the pillows were misplaced, and the writing table fell on the floor. Sameer slid through Aryakt's hands like sand sliding through the finger gaps.

"No, no. Don't touch those plants." Aryakt shouted.

"No no. I will." Sameer teased.

The three friends broke into a huge laughter. Settling down at their places after a few minutes, they felt the air light. Aryakt brought the lunch that he had cooked for his friends. As he served them in plates, he said:

"I never tried to talk to Bindu. Instead, you guys were behind her all the time. She spoke to me herself only once."

"Do not fake. Everyone in the school tried to talk to her," Sameer said.

"True. But now I am afraid that Aryakt never tried. Should be obvious, looking at him," signalled Madhava.

"But yes, I knew she wanted to talk to Aryakt. See, girls want to talk to you, man." Madhava continued.

"But this guy.... Here.... Don't understand the significance of it." Sameer added.

"Tell me one thing, Aryakt. Don't you think she was beautiful?" asked Madhava.

Aryakt's eyes became slightly more prominent. He could never control his blushing face. He tried to hold it this time and replied with some dignity, "Yes, she was. But how..........."

Sameer and Madhava got up from their chairs, instantly interrupting Aryakt, and lifted him on their shoulders.

"See how he is blushing. Still, he wants to behave like he has nothing for her."

The friends laughed thoroughly again.

"I should agree. She was extremely gorgeous." Aryakt said finally.

"Of course, of course," replied Madhava.

The lunch was tasty. The friends appreciated Aryakt's cooking skills, and after lunch, they returned to the day's topic. Aryakt was on his stubborn take on the topic.

Madhava thoughtfully said, "Please, Aryakt. It's for your good. We know you are happy with what you have. But please do this for *us*. You'll see it'll all be worth spending this time. Slowly, you'll be socially active. We want you to be socially welcome. The world is beautiful. We are here to explore. Do not miss that chance. At least try to get there. We are here to help you out. Please! Not that you are not aware of this thing, but...... "

Silence!

Aryakt, even though unwilling, had started imagining himself in the party that could bring around two hundred people together. He nodded more for Madhava's last reason than the party itself. His two friends didn't wait anymore since they didn't want Aryakt's mood to change. And they knew he'd make it to the party after his agreement.

As they descended the staircase, Aryakt smiled and waved at them.

"OH MY GOD!" he loudly exclaimed to himself.

❑

Chapter 3

The Party

The clock ticked 7 PM, and Aryakt felt his heart racing. The sweat all over his forehead was dripping down his cheeks and through his neck. He looked at himself in the mirror. As he was sure he must attend the party, he saw a warrior in the reflection. Taking a deep breath, he said to himself.

You can do this. Yes, it would help if you did this. Nothing is wrong with what Madhava and Sameer think. Could you do it for them? No, No. Could you do it for you? Something better is waiting for you.

He washed his face with soap and observed his eyes turning red in the crystal-clear mirror. He moved his head nearer to the mirror. *Will I see a different Aryakt from tomorrow? Will I be okay with this change in me? Tomorrow is Monday, and will my students be able to observe this change in me? What if I go mad in the party? What if I fall sick? What if I faint?*

He repeatedly splashed the cold water on his face to eliminate the popping thoughts. He then opened the almirah to find a new outfit nicely folded: a green GAP hoodie and a cream cargo. Aryakt remembered Madhava mentioning that he should wear a smart outfit. So, it should be their gift for him. He picked it up and wore it.

Looking at himself in the mirror, he recollected Mugdha's words that she said some months back. *Why don't you wear some trendy clothes? It'll suit you well.* He gave a regretful smile to himself and momentarily felt unhappy that the people around him were always concerned for him. With a wooden expression, he sat on the chair. The evening sea breeze ran over Vizag city in full swing. He stood on the terrace for a minute, prayed to God, took his wallet he had never used, locked the door, and got down from the two stored buildings. Every step he took down the stairs made him increasingly nervous.

He felt relieved, more than surprised to see Sameer waiting for him at the gate.

"Yay. You look great," said Sameer encouragingly.

This compliment made Aryakt's heart flutter, and that feeling of his manifested itself in the form of sweat on his forehead. He got into the car and remained silent with his head down. His evident worry was to keep himself unnoticed by the neighbourhood. Aryakt always thought that they might always notice his shy nature. Since he didn't speak to or even look at them while he walked through the streets, his behaviour could be easily misinterpreted as self-conceit. He was panicking to look around out of fear, imagining everyone laughing at his new *avatar*.

He kept squeezing his palms, thinking of the people around. He wanted to get out of the premises as soon as he could. Once the car crossed a few neighbouring lanes, Aryakt felt a little relieved since he had never walked in those lanes, and no one knew him even by face.

Sameer was always observing his panic but remained silent to give Aryakt time to settle down. Eventually, Sameer spoke:

"Don't panic. We'll be with you. And Madhava's relatives are very understanding. They mostly celebrate the functions in a 'not-so-loud' environment. It'll suit you. I fear you'll be bored at the function and if you feel so, try to talk to someone. You know, to pass the time. We'll be out by 10.30 PM or so. All fine?"

"Mmmm," said Aryakt in a shallow pitch of voice.

"Okay. Keep an eye on the food section. Once you see someone holding a food plate, we'll jump in, have food, and get out from the function once done. Fine?"

"Hmmm"

Sameer allowed Aryakt some time to figure out his thoughts. Meanwhile, he thought about the thing he lied to Aryakt. Sameer never knew how Madhava's relatives celebrate an essential function like 'Engagement.' Generally, people do not observe these kinds of occasions in silence. *What if they were very talkative? Never mind. They'll talk among themselves. Why would they bother Aryakt? What if they do bother? Madhava might not have yet told any of them about Aryakt's problem. What if Aryakt faints after an hour? Looking at him, it's entirely possible. No no. Why would he? We'll be with him. I am sure there'll not be much hungama. Just... Just some ceremonies. It should be fine. No. What if.....*

The friends heard loud drums as they approached the function hall. Sameer stopped the car well before the entrance. Aryakt and Sameer looked at the entrance keenly. They observed that every guest who arrived at the function was welcomed with the sounds of drums and other musical instruments. Around fifteen people, a mix of both genders hugged the guests and made them dance to the tunes. And only then are they allowed to get inside.

Sameer observed the scene with his mouth wide open. He then swallowed hesitantly.

Aryakt didn't blink his eyes and asked, "Are we at the right place?"

Sameer took his phone and checked the map Madhava shared with him. Yes, it was the right place.

"Yes", Sameer replied.

Aryakt was a person with stable thoughts despite his introverted nature. He never had these glitches before because he had never done anything that could make him uncomfortable. This was a monster situation for him. He could not deny going in because he never had ditched anyone. He thought about what worked the best to control his popping nerves. The things that fascinated him. He started speaking to himself, ensuring that his voice was quiet enough to be heard by Sameer. He murmured: *Physics. Non-linear dynamic problems. Oscillations. The book regarding self-motivation that Mugdha gave me. It was indeed good. Oh yes. Talking to myself - I learned from that book. There was another book from the same author, which was also noteworthy. It indeed dealt with social anxiety problems. It seemed almost written for me. So precise about what I feel. But I should learn to execute what I read from those inspirational books. Vilohith has an essay writing competition next week. Yes, he'll do well. And how about special relativity theory?*

Aryakt's state of mind was reflected in his eyes. They were red and tired almost. Sameer feared that the hosts might think Aryakt was drunk. He knew Madhava's family and relatives never encouraged alcohol consumption. He tapped on Aryakt's shoulder and said:

"Never mind. Everything is alright. Let's go in."

Sameer parked his car, and as Aryakt got out of that car, he could hear his heartbeat. As he approached the entrance, he realised that the rate at which it beat wasn't normal. It wouldn't be less than a hundred and twenty for sure.

Sameer felt the aura of fear himself while being around Aryakt. He realised that the fear was contagious. Suddenly, the drums sounded aloud. Sameer pulled himself out of the fear. The rhythm of the beat was so good that Sameer wanted to dance. He knew many of Madhava's relatives and almost everyone at the entrance. But Sameer didn't respond as he would have wished. Instead, he tried to comfort Aryakt by introducing him to the group. Aryakt tried to wish everyone well as Sameer introduced him. But he was murmuring something. They wished Aryakt back, and everyone encouraged the friends to dance. An aunty suddenly pulled Aryakt towards her and hugged him, understanding that he was Madhava's childhood friend.

Aryakt almost trembled.

"Come on, my kid. Dance!" said the hyperactive aunty.

As the drums were played, Aryakt said aloud at once, looking at her, "Simultaneity is not absolute. Light speed does not change, but time does since it is relative."

The hyperactive aunty's face turned pale. It was evident she didn't understand even a single word. But she followed Aryakt without hesitation. She said, "Yes. Yes. I am Madhava's relative. You are right."

She then held Aryakt's palms in hers and started dancing. Aryakt stood there, surrendering his hands to move as directed by that aunty.

Sameer, who was curiously observing Aryakt, was expressionless. He didn't notice that another hyperactive uncle was pushing him to dance. He desperately wanted to get rid of the group and get inside. It was unknown when Aryakt could burst out in tears or shout out the Arrhenius theory to that aunty.

Never in his life has Sameer danced so pathetically. There wasn't any sync between the beat of the drums and his dance.

Meanwhile, Madhava, in his cream-coloured blazer and blue cotton trousers, came out to the entrance expecting his friends. He laughed aloud, looking at Sameer's pathetic dance. Sameer took this chance to escape the hyperactive uncle and pulled Aryakt along. Sameer hugged Madhava as a gist of thankfulness for coming out for rescue.

"Is everything alright?" Madhava asked, looking at Sameer.

"Alright. Everything alright," Sameer said, trying to hide the uneasiness he felt for Aryakt. Aryakt, who still was murmuring something, followed his friends into the function hall.

The function was held on a big lawn decorated with lights and flowers, making the environment magnanimous. As they reached the lawn, Madhava took Sameer aside and said indicating to a group:

"Keep Aryakt away from that group of boys. They are a little upstart. The function will take some time to finish. It's yet to start, okay? Meanwhile, go upstairs if you want to look around the house. There will be people who you know. Take Aryakt along and introduce him."

Sameer looked at a group of four boys seated extremely casually and bursting into laughter once every two minutes. He then asked:

"Is this a house? I thought it is a function hall."

Madhava smiled and said, "No. Anu's dad owns a big business. This is his mansion."

Sameer said, "Alright," with an arched brow.

"I'll be around. Call me if needed." Madhava said and then spoke to Aryakt, giving him a dose of warm friendship and motivation.

Madhava left. Aryakt and Sameer occupied the last row of corner seats.

An announcement came from the stage before they could get themselves into the atmosphere around them.

"The engagement ceremony starts in another hour or so. Meanwhile, we have arranged a game for the guests. You need to write your names on a chit that'll be given to you now. The chits would be divided based on the gender. We'll pick one chit each from a group, and they should dance a minute on a duet song."

Almost everyone in the crowd cheered for the announcement.

These people are beyond my guess, Sameer thought.

One hour might have seemed too much for them, and this occasion was a relief – only for Sameer. He was excited for a moment, but his excitement decayed as he felt a hand on his shoulders. It was Aryakt, tensed.

"Let's move. We'll roam around," Aryakt said.

Sameer observed a frightening expression on Aryakt's face. Every coming minute seemed to have held a threatening remark on it for Aryakt. The current atmosphere around was blissful for any attendee but not for Aryakt. Sameer felt sad about his beloved friend's situation. Nevertheless, Aryakt had to face it. Sameer brought himself to control and said, "I'll write my name. You pretend to be writing and return an empty chit. So, you are out of it."

With his shivering lips, Aryakt said, "I can't sit here alone." Even though he didn't want Sameer to give up his excitement because of him.

"Well, okay. I'll also return an empty chit, then. Okay. Don't forget to fold it properly before returning," replied Sameer.

A girl ran across everyone with the chits, and another girl followed her and collected the chits with names written on them. As they both approached the friends, Aryakt got up suddenly and started walking swiftly towards the lawn exit.

The hyperactive aunty walking in saw Aryakt and got hold of him. She held his hand and took him to the first row of seats reserved for the core family members and VIPs.

Sameer ran along with Aryakt.

"Come. Come. Hello Ayesha. These two boys are Madhava's childhood friends. And they are seated in the last row. Did you guys write your name in it?"

"Not yet, mami," the two girls holding chits came forward.

"Well. Okay. Give three chits," the aunty said.

"Why three?" Sameer asked.

"Do you think I can't dance on a duet?" Aunty said aloud, looking at the guests.

The audience cheered aloud.

Aryakt, Sameer, and Sheela – three names written on the chits, and the girls segregated them.

Sameer hit his forehead with his palm, and to cover the gesture, he scratched it.

"Be seated. Be seated. Let's see how Ayesha is organising it."

Ayesha was the event organiser, and Sheela Aunty was the one who selected Ayesha for it. So, Ayesha had to be wonderful to be in Sheela Aunty's good books.

With increased energy, Ayesha gathered all the chits from the two girls.

Aryakt sat so uneasily that his situation looked as if a naughty, hyperactive teenager was punished for being seated single, silent, and hungry in a hot room during peak summer and watch back-to-back repeat shows of a dull Chinese documentary.

Sameer took his phone and called Madhava. No answer. He dialled again. No answer. Sameer messaged him – "Leave whatever you are doing and come near the stage immediately. Horrific things going on". The *danger* skull emoji followed.

The thick hoodie had to be saving Aryakt from the sea breeze, but instead, it made him feel suffocated. Aryakt wished to escape the function, remove his T-shirt, and run towards his house. Instead, he sat silently, took his handkerchief, and wiped the sweat on his face.

The first three chits didn't have Aryakt's name on it. But the fourth chit had it. The girl was a young and lovely-looking Varsha. Probably the most beautiful girl in the whole function. After seeing some dreadful performances in the first three minutes, guests were waiting for an entertaining act.

Aryakt's legs started shivering. Sameer requested the aunty not to force Aryakt to get onto the stage.

"Please Sheela Aunty. Do not force him. He is not doing good these days. If you want, I can go instead of him."

Sheela Aunty looked at him and said, "Aaahaaan!! I know why you want to go. Varsha on the other side. Don't be too smart, mister. Let Aryakt go. He looks handsome. Your chance, too, would come, probably with me."

"Oh no," Sameer murmured.

Sheela Aunty held Sameer's hand tight so that he stayed where he was.

Varsha got onto the stage. Aryakt sat with his head down. Sheela Aunty started screaming.

"Aryakt.. Aryakt....Aryakt"

The entire crowd started shouting in rhythm. Aryakt's innocent behaviour made everyone like him on the first go. With the scream of Aryakt's name, Madhava ran to the lawn.

A boy from the guests came forward and forcibly made Aryakt get up and walk to the stage. He fumbled on the staircase. He got himself up and finally onto the stage. Varsha came and stood beside him.

If the timid nature of Aryakt was kept aside for a moment, he looked equally dashing beside Varsha. His lack of confidence caused his handsomeness to break apart.

A super hit number from the Telugu movie Kushi was played. Guests cheered and sang the song in chorus. Varsha started moving a little, but Aryakt, with his head down, was standing still, twisting his palms.

Sheela Aunty got onto the stage and tried to make Aryakt dance. While Aryakt tried to get away from her, they ended up being at the edge of the stage and Sheela Aunty fell on the thick grass of the lawn. Standing near the stage, Sameer tried to hold her, but he couldn't.

She landed with a bent ankle on the ground. She could realise instantly that she probably had her ankle sprained. The guests jumped forward and made her sit on a chair.

The ankle pain was quite evident after around five minutes. One of the organising team members brought a pain relief and sprayed it on her ankle. After a minute, she felt relieved and looked around for Aryakt. He wasn't there anywhere on the lawn.

❑

Chapter 4

Sameer and Madhava ran around to find Aryakt. Madhava mentioned that Aryakt would try to get home. So, they rushed to the exit gate and saw Aryakt speaking to the security guard.

Aryakt saw them approaching him. He tried to run away. Madhava ran and got hold of him.

"Hello, Aryakt. Why are you running away? Where are you going?" asked Madhava.

Aryakt desperately wanted to get out of the scene, he pulled Madhava towards him, and said in a low-pitched voice, "I am running to save my life. I am done for the day. Please don't force me anymore."

"Well. Well. What happened? Sheela Aunty sprained her ankle. It could be a fracture."

Sameer finally came to his senses and said, "She was trying to get you into the act."

"I understand Sameer. She does not know my problem, but you guys do. I cannot take it anymore."

Aryakt looked restless, but he wasn't panicking. Madhava looked at Sameer and winked. He then said, "Fine then. Sameer will drop you home. But don't you think you should at least apologise to Sheela Aunty?"

Aryakt thought momentarily and said, "No. I cannot come in at any cost. You convey my apologies to her. And I can go home by myself." and started walking and got out from the exit gate.

Sameer and Madhava stood helpless and disappointed.

"Whatever he had gone through in last twenty minutes or so was..........." Sameer half smiled and nodded his head.

Madhava said understandingly, "Let us try some other time. I wished him to stay back for some more time. It'll be good for him. But poor Sheela Aunty. She sprained her ankle."

Suddenly, they saw Aryakt running towards them from the exit gate. The premises were lightly illuminated since the exit time was nowhere near. He said hurriedly, "I think you are right, Maddy. I should... I should be sorry about what happened to Sheela Aunty. And I am. Do you think I should let her know this myself?"

The last sentence came out ambivalently.

Madhava looked at him keenly and felt a ray of hope. He smiled and said, "Yes. Absolutely."

As they walked in, Madhava said, "For what you have done, Aryakt, you should be careful now. Have your fear in control."

Sameer patted Madhava's shoulder for the comment.

The word *fear* had triggered itself inherently in Aryakt. He said, trying to bring his fear under control, "Okay. It'll take just two minutes to say a sorry, or probably one."

Sheela Aunty was back to form, and the lawn returned to its delightful atmosphere. As the three friends approached Sheela Aunty, they saw a boy drawing something on a whiteboard placed on the stage. It was the dumb charades game going on.

"Hey Aryakt. Where did you go? We were missing you." Sheela Aunty said in excitement, looking at Aryakt.

Everyone looked at Aryakt with an unpleasant expression except Sheela Aunty. She pulled him and got him seated on the chair beside her. Aryakt sat holding his hands and legs tight.

Madhava and Sameer sat on the chairs across the other side. Sameer looked at Sheela Aunty in surprise. *What did she have to do with Aryakt? Why is she so kind to him?*

"Bajrangi Bhaijaan," someone shouted from among the guests.

Everyone clapped for the correct answer. Aryakt got up to say sorry to Sheela Aunty.

"It's Aryakt's turn now," shouted Sheela Aunty.

Madhava and Sameer whistled aloud. The guests joined them by clapping.

The host, Ayesha, got down the stage as she knew Aryakt would be too shy to come onto the stage himself.

"Careful, this time." shouted one of the guests.

Aryakt looked at his friends with desperate gestures. His eyes reflected the distressed situation.

Ayesha showed a chit to Aryakt on which a movie name was written. Aryakt didn't know about the game, and he looked lost. He didn't have any idea about the movie title he just read. As guests started chattering, the boys seated at the back started laughing aloud and commenting.

Ayesha explained the game to Aryakt, and sweat rolled down his neck as expected. He was innocently nodding his head for everything that she said.

"Please ensure that anything you write or draw shouldn't be obvious. It should be an indirect way of representation, you know!"

"Fine. But I do not have any knowledge about movies." Aryakt said in a shallow pitch of voice.

"Okay. But the audience has. That's the challenge. Go ahead."

"What's the name of the movie?"

Ayesha showed him the chit again and moved to the other side of the stage. Aryakt looked confused. A whiteboard and himself in front of it wasn't new for him. But the occasion was unique. It wasn't a class that he taught to his students. Around a hundred people were in front of him. As the ceremony time was nearing, many guests gathered on the lawn. The glittering sarees, the perfect suits, the smiling faces – all were looking at Aryakt.

He just stood thinking. The last row of boys started commenting.

"Got any idea of throwing someone else from the stage?" a boy from the group shouted.

"Give him some time, guys." Sheela Aunty answered.

After a very uncomfortable moment, Aryakt closed his eyes and took a deep breath. Wiping the sweat from the forehead and neck, he took the marker placed in front of the board. He assumed himself to be in his home. He forgot about the gathering. He ignored the comments. Thinking about his favourite book, he spoke to himself - quietly this time. Madhava and Sameer held each other's hands, looking at Aryakt getting into the act.

Aryakt wrote $CaCO_3$ on the board and just stood facing it. He didn't have enough courage to turn towards the guests.

"It is for us to see, not for you," the same boy shouted.

Aryakt rubbed it and wrote it in a big font this time – $CaCO_3$

The guests laughed aloud in synchronisation. Sameer and Madhava looked at each other surprisingly. Sameer then whistled aloud. Madhava, too, couldn't control his laughter.

"Is it a chemistry class or something?" someone said.

"Professor," someone guessed the answer.

"Taaren zameen par," someone else shouted.

"In that case, *he* should be that boy in the film." Someone said. Madhava and Sameer felt terrible about it. However, Aryakt couldn't understand anything about the comment.

Ayesha, who looked most confused about why he wrote it, couldn't come to her senses yet. She suddenly brought herself into the moment when people shouted various titles and requested the guests to repeat their answers. None was the correct answer.

"Can you draw something else instead?"

Aryakt thought for a moment and tried to draw a face resembling a person with *pagdi*. It wasn't a padgi exactly. But it resembled it.

Someone from the crowd shouted, "Bhaag Milkha Bhaag"

Ayesha said "No" and encouraged that person to guess other titles. People understood that the title should be on the lines of some sports.

"Lagaan" someone shouted.

"No," Ayesha replied and continued, "Time over. Time over."

The guests felt disappointed. Ayesha asked Aryakt to say the answer.

He said it aloud, "Chak de India."

"Ooooh!" guests shouted.

Sheela Aunty asked him as he was about to get down the stage. "What did you try to write and draw? How is it linked to the title or the movie?"

Ayesha added. "I didn't get what clue you were trying to give."

Madhava and Sameer looked keenly at Aryakt. They knew some peculiar and unique explanation was on its way. Ayesha held the mike near Aryakt.

Aryakt said, "This is Sir C.V. Raman, who won the Nobel prize for his *Raman effect*. He is from India. So..."

"That is a weird way of conveying it," said a gentleman seated beside Madhava.

"And what's that chemistry mister hoodie?" asked the backbencher.

Madhava held Sameer's hand tightly and said, "He'll shoot now."

Aryakt said, "It's Calcium carbonate – the chemical formula for Chalk that we use to write on a blackboard. It resembled the *Chak* word."

Madhava and Sameer stood up from the chair and whistled aloud.

"There you are to know Mr. Aryakt. An excellent teacher. A wonderful teacher. I hope you all learned something new tonight. And dear students, whoever is here, Aryakt teaches various subjects at his home. Regardless of what stream you are studying in. I can give you his phone number if you wish to consult him."

If not for Madhava's backup, the moment would have resulted in heavy laughter and almost humiliation for Aryakt. Instead, Madhava turned it all into a moment where people appreciated Aryakt.

As the appreciation was frightening for him, he broke into a sweat again and silently got down from the stage.

The ceremony started in another fifteen minutes as the close guests, including Sheela Aunty, entered the stage. The bride and bridegroom were brought onto the stage as the Indian traditional music – Sannayi was played.

Sameer and Aryakt sat at the same place where they had previously been seated. After around half an hour, as the ceremony was over, people started to get to the stage for a photograph with the new couple. Aryakt remembered Sameer's words that he said when they started from his home.

He looked around excitedly and saw some older people holding the food plates. He smiled, feeling the gist of relief to get home soon.

"Sameer, let's go and have dinner," he requested.

"You wait here. I'll go and give the gift to the couple. If you want, you can join." Said Sameer, getting up from his chair.

"No. Please!!"

"Well, wait then. Please!" said Sameer and quickly walked towards the stage.

Sameer somehow managed to keep Aryakt away from the photograph session since he knew that Aryakt had enough for the day.

Informing Madhava over the phone, they started having their dinner. It was a buffet arrangement on another lawn opposite the ceremony.

Sheela Aunty emerged onto the lawn as they were about to finish eating. Looking at the two friends, she exclaimed, "Hello Aryakt. That was a funny way of conveying 'chak.' Have a peaceful dinner. I'll get my plate," and swiftly walked to the dining section.

"Let's move quickly before she is back. I am almost done with the dinner," Aryakt said.

Sheela Aunty stopped, turned back, looked at Aryakt, and said, "We have another quick game after dinner. Don't even think of going back home until it's done."

Aryakt looked at Sheela Aunty's swinging ponytail as she walked toward the dining section. *What kind of a person she is?* He thought.

Aryakt looked pale suddenly and developed a cold sweat. The nauseous feeling had overridden his patience. He dropped the plate on the floor and started running randomly throughout the lawn. Guests were confused by his behaviour. Sameer left his plate on a table and started running behind Aryakt.

"This guy is a nuisance." said the backbencher, looking at his friends.

❑

Chapter 5

Sameer understood that Aryakt was about to throw up. He remembered Madhava's advice to get into the room on the first floor in case of any need. He took Aryakt along with him to the first floor.

Sameer knocked on the door, but no one answered. He pushed it with force, and it, at once, swung open. Without making any noise, he searched for a washroom, and it was there attached to the bedroom. Since no one was in the room, he indicated the washroom to Aryakt and got himself out of the main hall. He stood in the first-floor corridor, viewing the beautiful sight of the two lawns.

He tried calling Madhava, but the call went unanswered.

Aryakt vomited most of his food in the bathtub. He could never spot the washbasin that was hidden behind the door. To clean the bathtub, he tried opening the tap which was latched to the shower.

A rush of cold water coming out of the shower drenched him entirely before he realised how to turn off the shower. After a bit of analysis of the pipeline system (in his mind), he could figure out how to latch it for the tap. He cleaned the bathtub hurriedly and shivered with his wet hoodie and cargo jeans.

He got out of the washroom, looking for Sameer. Instead, he saw a girl hooking her blouse on her back. She wore a black transluscent saree and a sleeveless blouse with diamond-like stones surrounding the entire circumference. The saree was carved with many shining stones that glittered in his eyes. The 'pallu' was lying on the carpet floor. She was looking at the mirror, and Aryakt was standing behind her, facing her.

She noticed someone behind her back and turned around in shock. It was Varsha.

"What the hell are you doing here?" she shouted.

Aryakt jumped at once and replied, "I was wearing a saree while its pallu was on the floor, and when I vomited and hooked the blouse at the back, the handle, unknown to me, was latched to the shower instead of the tap. And while I figured out the black saree, which shined like a diamond, I couldn't help myself since it was glittering in my eyes. And it drenched me totally with cold water."

Even though she was at her peak anger, Varsha couldn't resist laughing aloud.

"Have you gone mad?" she asked, still laughing.

"No, no. Let me put it clearly. When I was eating, Sheela Aunty's blouse was hooked from the back, and the pallu was on the floor. I figured out how the pipeline must have been designed to handle the shower and tap with a single knob. But Sameer brought me here since the saree was glittering in my eyes."

"Alright. Alright. Take a break. Have a seat in the other room. I'll be there." She closed the door behind Aryakt, and he sat on a chair in the other room, following Varsha's instruction.

After a few minutes, she was back and saw Aryakt shiver while the air conditioning was at eighteen degrees. She switched off the air conditioner and gave him a towel to wipe himself. As he did so, Sameer opened the door and saw Aryakt wiping his hair with a towel and Varsha looking gorgeous beside him.

His surprise was quite evident in his expression.

"What is going on here?" he asked.

"Ask your friend. I am going down for dinner. Catch you there." She said and walked out of the room. She stopped at once, turned back, and continued, "Do not explain him in the same way you did to me."

After Varsha left the room, Sameer looked at Aryakt, laughed in surprise, and asked, "What is going on here, Aryakt? What did you do?"

Aryakt and Sameer sat on either side of Sheela Aunty, helpless. Madhava came to Sameer and surprisingly asked, "How did you end up here? And I hope you had dinner."

"You do not pick up my call during critical times; later, you show up and ask questions. What an unschooled behaviour, Maddy!"

"What happened?" Madhava asked concerningly.

"Leave that story. But see....." Sameer indicated toward Sheela Aunty and said in a shallow voice, "Let us get Aryakt out of here. Look at him. He is on the verge of going mad, literally."

"Wait. Let me see what's going on here." Madhava said and went to Ayesha to understand what the game was.

He came back to Sheela Aunty, sat on his knees beside her, and said softly, "Hey, Sheela kaki! The game is to perform on the stage. I mean for whatever talent you possess. I think... I think you should let Aryakt.... And Sameer go. It is getting late for them to reach home."

"I understand Madhava beta. They needn't worry. I can drop them in my car if they fear going alone." She looked at Aryakt and asked, "Are you afraid of going home, baccha?"

Aryakt stopped thinking about what he was afraid of. He was going with the flow. He had surrendered himself to Sheela Aunty's thoughts.

"I don't know," he said, being very soft.

Meanwhile, Ayesha announced the start of the game. The bride and bridegroom were the ones to start with. They danced in a duet for a minute, and the auditorium sang the song in chorus.

The backbencher then danced to a peppy Bollywood number. Another group of boys danced to Pawan Kalyan's song. The guests, as expected, shouted, "Power Star! Power Star!"

"The last chance before we end the game," announced Ayesha.

Sheela Aunty got up excitedly. "Here is the last performance," she said, pulling Aryakt to get up from his chair.

"No. No. No. Please don't push him any further. We don't have an ambulance ready here." Sameer said straight on the face of Sheela Aunty.

"I have my car ready. Don't worry," she replied sharply.

"Go, baccha. Go. I am here. Don't worry. Let us see what happens." she encouraged Aryakt.

Tired, Aryakt had to take on another battle of the day. He got onto the stage, taking baby steps.

"Chemistry class starts now." Shouted the backbencher.

Aryakt took the mike from Ayesha as she offered it hesitantly. "Are you going to sing?" she asked.

He went a little close to her and said, "I know I'll have to do this. I can't escape anyhow. I want to finish it fast."

"Great. Go on," Ayesha replied.

Aryakt's shivering hands tried to hold the mike well. He never had spoken into it at any time.

In his shivering tone, he said, "I would like to read out something that I wrote for a special person."

Madhava and Sameer looked at each other with narrowed eyes.

"Go ahead! Go ahead!" shouted Sheela Aunty.

Aryakt wiped his sweat from the forehead and neck. He then tried to recollect something. Hesitant to look at the audience, he read out his mind.

Once in a while,

Do not blame me for forgetting to walk late at night because I see your eyes in the sparkling stars!

Do not blame me for forgetting to visit a beach because I see your thoughts in the plunging waves!

Do not blame me when I forget to touch the grass because I see your courage in how it emerges!

Do not blame me when I forget to light a lamp because I see your glowing smile in the brightening air!

Do not blame me when I forget to help those in need because I see your personality in their smile!

Do not blame me when I don't read a book because I see your life in the progressing story!

And always,

Blame me for not visiting the Amazon rain forest every day to feel the blossom of that orchid flower hidden in the dense dark green leaves without enough sunlight and never noticed by anyone, but still blooming because I see the 'complete' you in its every petal!

The guests went lull for a moment. There was a pin-drop silence around. Madhava and Sameer looked at the guests, wondering.

Silence!

Sheela Aunty got up from her chair and started clapping.

The guests then clapped hesitantly.

"Did *you* write this?" asked Varsha, seated in the first row on the other side.

"Yes," Aryakt answered, avoiding eye contact with her, as the claps continued.

"Who is that girl for whom you wrote this?" asked the backbencher sarcastically.

"I wrote it for my mom," Aryakt replied plainly.

Silence!

"Mom?" Varsha asked.

"Yes. I don't remember seeing my mom at all. But..... But I would have felt this for her had she been alive with me."

Silence!

"Can you reread it? My... Our perspective the whole time was that the poem was for your girlfriend or someone you love," said Varsha.

"Yes, it is for someone I love. My mother."

Aryakt read it out again.

The auditorium erupted with claps and cheers of the guests. The bride and bridegroom got onto the stage again to take a photograph with Aryakt. This time, Aryakt was in the centre.

Sameer and Madhava were excitedly punching the air with ecstatic tears in their eyes.

Sheela Aunty hugged Aryakt as he got down the stage. But he wasn't reacting to anything. Madhava and Sameer shook hands with him happily.

Looking at Aryakt, Sameer indicated that it was time to leave. Madhava agreed. Sheela Aunty nodded.

Madhava indicated Aryakt and Sameer to leave. Aryakt stopped at once, got to Sheela Aunty, and said, "I feel sorry that you sprained your ankle because of me. It might cause pain later. For the kind of landing, I think you might have small tears in the Calcaneofibular ligament. Can you forgive me?"

Sheela raised her eyebrows, smiled, and said, "Of course. It wasn't your mistake unless you deliberately took me to the edge of the stage." She then laughed aloud. After making the air light, Sheela Aunty said goodbye and got herself to the other guests.

Leaving Sameer and Madhava, Aryakt had to get to the washroom. As he swiftly walked, there was a guest room where he saw some girls singing and dancing.

He suddenly saw something that made him feel shocked. *Who was that dancing?*

He couldn't hold himself back as he thought about the name, and the impact of the evening's proceedings captured his thoughts again. Realising that the name he thought about was almost making him panic, the nausea got to its peak, and he vomited again. The stress of the evening was clearly showing up in his eyes.

Sameer and Aryakt started to go to Aryakt's home by car, and Aryakt looked indifferent by his expression.

In the auditorium, as everyone was getting ready to leave, Madhava sat beside Sheela Aunty and said:

"Thank you, Sheela Kaki. Thanks a lot for your help. I could believe only you. Whatever you did was cornering Aryakt, but it was for his good. Thanks for helping us out."

"Why do you say that? When you told me about Aryakt yesterday, I assumed I was in his shoes; it wouldn't be easy for me either. But your plan of making him get onto the stage time and again was a good one. Aryakt is a lovely boy. He'll be alright. He should be proud to have a friend like you, Madhava." Said Sheela Aunty, holding Madhava's hand.

"Rather, it's the other way around. Sameer and I are proud and lucky to have a friend like Aryakt. He is the best. He lags in his confidence – that's it. No one knows him well. Not many know him at all. He does not have any appreciation from anyone, but he should have been getting all the appreciation for his very nature. Only a mother can see *that* greatness in her child at times. Aryakt has no one who has that soft corner for him. His life is empty. Thanks for playing the role of his mother." Madhava said, recollecting his mother, whom he lost a couple of years back.

Sheela Aunty patted his shoulder and gave an understanding nod.

Sheela Aunty and Madhava deserved a cold mango milkshake. They had it seated on the lawn.

❑

Chapter 6

On the way home, Aryakt sat silently and thought about the dance he saw. He knew that the instant by itself didn't stand as a delinquent act. However, many popping thoughts flooded his mind. Sameer wanted to speak to him and ensure that everything was alright. He believed that Aryakt didn't realise that he had broken some barriers during the party for his own good. Aryakt certainly deserved a standing ovation. Suddenly, Aryakt started breathing heavily, and the sweat filled his face.

Sameer immediately stopped the car to check Aryakt. His skin was icy, and his eyes weren't looking as usual. He turned the car towards the nearest multi-specialty hospital.

The nurse staff took Aryakt into the emergency ward, and the duty doctor did a primary checkup. The blood pressure had dropped to deficient levels. The doctor's opinion of its cause was reduced energy and dehydration.

Aryakt was given some medication and was asked to be there in the emergency ward for at least five hours to monitor his blood pressure. The doctor wanted to ensure it was a temporary dip due to the stress.

Sameer telephoned Madhava, and he immediately rushed to the hospital. The friends waited outside the hospital till morning.

At around 5 AM, Aryakt's blood pressure was stable, and he was asked to get home with some blood tests suggested. Madhava paid the hospital bill.

The three friends started to Aryakt's home in Sameer's car. Madhava was casual to keep Aryakt from getting overwhelmed by the happenings of the evening and night.

"Who am I? What is my identity? Why should people care about me?" Aryakt said, staring at his lap. He was seated beside Sameer. Sitting in the back seat, Madhava bent forward and kept his hand on Aryakt's shoulder.

"Please, Aryakt," Madhava said, but Aryakt interrupted him.

"I can't even pay my hospital bill even in an emergency. Why should you, being my friend, pay for it? Why should you do anything for me? Am I doing anything for you guys?" Aryakt was shooting his questions, probably to himself. He continued:

"And she... Sheela Aunty. Why does she bother about me? She saw me only today and behaved like she had known me forever. She tries to keep me in the limelight. Why should she bother about me?"

"She was trying to......." Madhava interrupted.

"I know... I know..!" Aryakt continued, "I know she was trying to help me. But what did she get back? A sprain in her ankle?"

"The world is being nice to me. Very nice. But I am not nice, even to myself. Leave apart about what I am giving back to the world. Now, you see. Sameer and you are bothered about me the whole time during the party. Sameer left his duet dance opportunity, probably with that beautiful girl."

Sameer raised his eyebrows (probably remembering Varsha) and brought them down again instantly.

"And these clothes. You gifted it to me. But do I stand a chance, or am I worth wearing this? And first of all, why should you gift it to me? Will I be able to buy this myself even after, say, five years from now? Capability-wise, No. Intention wise, No."

"I am a born loser. What if I read those excellent motivational books? The intent would still be the same. Live my life alone. Strive to pay the bills. Be afraid of people. The authors talk about motivation. Where will I find it? Do I want to find it? The answer is a big No. I am... I am used to living a life like this. I am happy with it, Madhava. I am happy with it. I haven't paid my rent for the last two months. And the owner never asks me about it. I feel more guilty when he does not remind me or ask me for it. How do I come out of this financial situation? I am not happy about it. I can live as an introvert alone, but not with financial bottlenecks at every juncture. You know, if I think about being in your shoes, I'll give up on the efforts to try to change a person like Aryakt. Because....... Because I don't feel that I am losing anything here being an introvert. I know there are many introverts out there. But yes, no one would be like me. With such a reluctance to mingle in the society. But the problem is, I am happy with it."

Madhava and Sameer just listened to Aryakt silently the whole time. They were sad about Aryakt's situation. It was terrifying for them to understand that Aryakt was quite happy being disconnected from the world. But they were pleased that he was wishing for money. Financial crisis - one of the big reasons to be worried or at least concerned about. *But how does he earn it? What would motivate him?*

As they reached Aryakt's home, Aryakt said, "Please stop the car here, Sameer. I'll sit here on this chair for some time. If you want to go home, then please do so."

"No. We'll wait for you at your house. Give me the room keys," said Madhava.

"It's beneath the yellow rose flowerpot. Fourth from the left of the door." Aryakt said and continued:

"Oh, wait. It's 6 AM already. Kids might have opened the door and sat inside. I'll come in sometime."

"Alright." Sameer parked the car, and they walked the staircase to the penthouse.

Aryakt sat on the metal chair, thinking about the present situation. He was happy till the last morning. *Does this party change the whole circumstance for him? Probably, yes. Was it for good? Probably, yes. Was he ready to change his mind-set and leave his comfort zone? A big no.*

He kept his head down as always. Lifting it will make him see the people around him. He did it deliberately only when someone called him for some purpose, which was quite unlikely to happen. He only lifted his head when he wanted to purchase something. It would be for a couple of seconds.

After some time, as he felt the known air aroma around him and tried to settle his thoughts, a gust of sea breeze overlapped the surroundings. To set right his hair, Aryakt lifted his head and saw his students, along with Sameer and Madhava, standing at the terrace's railing.

After listening to the party proceedings, Mugdha was surprised and said, "I was at that party. The bridegroom, Balu, is my cousin."

"What?!" Sameer asked in surprise.

Mugdha stayed silent, looking at Sameer and Madhava alternately with widened eyes. Madhava thoughtfully paused, silent for a minute. Meanwhile, Sameer asked:

"Where were you? When did you come? I... We did''t see you there. Were you on the lawn where the ceremony took place?"

Before Mugdha could answer, Madhava asked, "Did you see Aryakt? Or did he see you?"

"No. I didn't see him. I am not sure if he saw me or not?"

Madhava said, looking at Mugdha, "I think you all should get home now. He is not in a mood to teach."

Sameer nodded in agreement.

As the kids started leaving, seemingly disappointed, Mugdha took a book from her bag and gave it to Madhava.

"It's another book from a series that sir was interested in reading. Can you please give it to him?"

Madhava nodded and took it. The students started walking down the stairs with their heads down.

Madhava observed the title *Perceive the deceiving 'Impossible' – by aNoNyMuOs*.

"Interesting," he remarked.

Chapter 7

Even after two days, Aryakt needed to be entirely into his routine. The impact of *that* night wasn't going away anytime soon. Though Aryakt's confidence altered, his financial situation made him depressed. Variation in blood pressure, which could happen due to overstress, was enough to shuttle his financials and make him helpless.

One day, around 5.30 AM, Aryakt locked the door of his room and walked onto the main road of Seetamma dhaara to get some vegetables for the coming two days. He always ensured he got all his groceries before the world woke up fully. The only vegetable vendor available then knew that Aryakt never came to him during other times of the day. It took him around half an hour to get back home.

He took his phone to turn off the alarm for the next day, which he had set to bring the vegetables. It startled him as he saw five missed calls. All were from the same phone number of the 'Venkoba Rao Trust Hospital.' Apart from some customer care calls and calls from Sameer or Madhava, no one else telephoned Aryakt.

His heart started racing, anticipating some news from the hospital. His only blood relative – his grandfather was in a coma for the last twenty-two years. Aryakt never remembered talking to his grandfather. However, as he reflected on the slight remembrance of his grandfather's smile, he could only recollect his pale, white face with a thin white beard at the chin. Aryakt used to visit the hospital once every three months. Thinking of his grandfather comforted him and he was not nervous speaking to his grandfather - like what he felt while talking to the kids. But his grandfather's face always made him tense. Behind those closed eyes, he believed his grandfather was waiting to tell him something, as if someone had held his throat tight, stopping him from talking. Aryakt thought that the old man held himself from shouting out. But the day he wakes up might be unusual, as Aryakt could sense. Momentous.

Aryakt never had extended his thoughts further. He made himself unintentionally comfortable with the expression of his grandfather, which reminded him of a highly excited old man who was forced to be silent. A volcano is waiting to erupt, waiting for a crack in that probable vent.

The phone rang again, and it was from the hospital. Aryakt's hands shivered as his mind thought of various possibilities. Another dreadful situation for him was talking to an unknown person over the phone, focusing on the words, and replying consciously. It wasn't the kind of call where you can disconnect, saying just 'not interested.'

He took the call trembling and tried to portray himself as in control. It was a nurse on the other side. Her voice was lovely and childlike.

"Is it Mr. Aryakt?"

"Yes," Aryakt said.

"This is to inform you that around one hour back, Mr. Srivatsa, your grandfather had shown some sign of movement, and his pulse and heartbeat are in control. Can you be here in the hospital as soon as you can?"

Aryakt couldn't believe what she said on the first go. But then he rephrased the words, felt them, and said, "Yes."

"Thank you." The nurse said and disconnected the call.

Aryakt thanked God that he could get away with just two yeses.

'Handling a situation' wasn't the most likely thing that Aryakt had done in his life. On the contrary, it was the most unlikely encounter (thanks to Madhava and Sameer for risking their reputation and forcibly taking him to the party).

He had a humongous task of getting to the hospital and handling the situation. He wasn't sure if he was happy listening to the fact that his grandfather might wake up again and talk to him or if he was tense that a long-lasting silence might break. *What does that mean? It could mean a person, it could mean a family, it could mean happiness, and it could mean a change. Was he ready for a change?* It is a tricky circumstance when one is reluctant to absorb the awaited happiness only because it brings in a *change* along with it. Aryakt understood a bit more about himself. He wasn't excited about it, though.

Aryakt consolidated all the cash with him, anticipating some expenses at the hospital. He had never taken a city bus in his entire life to travel intracity destinations. He walked to most of the destinations. Recollecting that the nurse had asked him to come to the hospital as soon as possible, he took an auto-rickshaw and thought about the motivational book that Mugdha had given him. It said something about humans' deception during every stage of their life. Something that seems impossible is always a deception. Any deception should be counter-acted; the minutest effort towards counteraction could bring significant results.

❑

Chapter 8

Venkoba Rao Trust was a medium-scale hospital that accommodated around fifty in-patients at its maximum. Mr. Srivatsa was admitted to it on the compassionate grounds that he served the Indian army for more than ten years.

With absolute uncertainty regarding what could happen in the hospital, Aryakt entered the lawn, which was neatly maintained. A small water fountain added a serene beauty to the perfectly trimmed bushes fencing the yard. After taking a few deep breaths and talking to himself (murmuring about how methanol could stop the water from freezing), Aryakt entered the hospital and enquired at the reception.

He was guided to the second floor, where the nurse, Mrs. Gowri, who telephoned him, greeted him warmly.

"Doctor Garg will talk to you in a while. Please be seated here." She said as she guided him to Dr. Garg's consulting room.

Aryakt was seated, squeezing his hands and trying to control his heart, which was brutally hitting the ribs. His anticipations wandered everywhere. *Is his grandfather awake yet? Did something happen to him?* The situation was overwhelming for him to take it alone. Immediately, he took the phone and thought of calling Madhava. He discarded the thought since his two friends had had enough during and after the party. He didn't want to give them any trouble for the week, at least.

Thinking of the motivational book, he sat up straight, decided to take whatever came, and took a couple of deep breaths as the door clutched open and Dr. Garg entered the room. He was six feet tall, fair, and handsome, around forty-five years of age. He wished Aryakt with a great smile. The confidence that Dr. Garg presented had shattered Aryakt's leftover confidence, and he entered his usual comfort zone of being anxious. Sweat started popping up on his forehead.

"Are you the only relative of Mr. Srivatsa?" asked Dr. Garg enquiringly.

"Yes," Aryakt replied in alertness.

"See, let me be clear on one thing, Mr. Aryakt. Your grandfather is eighty-six years old now, and he has been in a coma for around twenty-two years now, which is quite a rare occurrence in medical history. The moment deserves to be in the news, I wonder," he continued, explaining with his hyper-excited expression that diminished Aryakt's left-out confidence.

"This morning, our nurse had observed a movement in his eyes and fingers. The pulse rate and blood pressure have been in the range expected in coma patients. Even half an hour back, there was a physical movement. We are monitoring his pulse and other parameters continuously. But I should say one thing to you. If he happened to wake up anytime soon, then it'll be a critical case for us to handle. It'll depend on how he responds. Anything might happen. Hope you understand."

Aryakt's expressionless face was understandable for the doctor. Understandingly, he said:

"If you want to stay here for some time, you may. Otherwise, we'll call you if there is an update. I should go on rounds now. You can sit here if you want."

Dr. Garg left the room, which led to a quietus.

After fifteen minutes of embarrassed silence in the room and a cluster of thoughts that Aryakt fought with, the door again clutched open. This time, it was a hurried sound. It was Mrs. Gowri, the nurse, who rushed into the room.

"Mr. Srivatsa opened his eyes. Do you want to see him?" she asked hurriedly.

Aryakt felt an explosion in his mind, and his heart raced like a cheetah. He was about to cry out of panic. He took his phone and again discarded the thought of calling Madhava or Sameer. His hands were shivering, and he felt that he could faint at any moment. He held Mrs. Gowri's hand and requested her to wait. She felt his freezing palms and offered a glass of water.

Even though Aryakt never discloses the problem he always suffered from, he did this time. One can hold one's psychological conscience to a limit. As the breaking point nears, every human around is the same. He said in a low-pitched voice, "I have extreme social anxiety, and I cannot even talk to any unknown person. It's not that I can't talk, but I feel extremely anxious looking at people and people looking at me. The thing you told me is making me very, you know..."

Mrs. Gowri interrupted him, made him sit on the chair, kept her hand on his shoulders, and said, "Calm down. I know what social anxiety is. I am here with you. Okay. Do not worry. We are all here with you."

Understanding that Aryakt does not have any of his family members, Mrs. Gowri felt sad for him and an obvious need to be around him for some time. Looking at Aryakt's confused expression, she couldn't determine if he was excited or anxious about the news.

"Do you want to see your grandfather? You need not talk to him. Just look at him once, as I am sure you have not seen him with his eyes open. You know, he is your family. Are you excited?" she said encouragingly.

❑

Chapter 9

Aryakt got up from the chair unwillingly. As they moved towards the Intensive Care Unit, where Mr. Srivatsa was shifted that morning and was the only patient there, Aryakt was only thinking about the motivational book. The war he was fighting in his mind was the one the world would ridicule. Yet, he had to fight it.

Mr. Srivatsa looked bloodless and pale. His whitish eyes looked dull as he stared at emptiness towards the ceiling. Mrs. Gowri held Aryakt's palm and placed it on his grandfather's hand. The wrinkled hand with popped-up nerves was skinny, and Aryakt felt the cold touch of his grandfather's skin. Aryakt and the nurse stayed there for a couple of minutes, and the nurse, in a low-pitched voice, broadcasted, "Mr. Srivatsa. Can you hear me? It's your grandson, Aryakt. Can you feel his palm on your hands?"

No response. Aryakt looked at Mrs. Gowri with a flat expression.

"Do you want to talk to him?" she asked.

Aryakt didn't know the answer to it. Considering the circumstance, he thought, *Maybe, no*.

The man in front of him was the one who probably would have taken Aryakt in his lap during his childhood. The one who probably loved him with his whole heart. The one who probably taught him how to talk. Two big tears rolled down Aryakt's eyes when he thought about it. All this while he was thinking about his problem, but when he felt from his grandfather's perspective, he couldn't control his tears. He felt his heart melting.

What would he be talking to me if he woke up? Will he be able to observe anything? Will he be able to remember that he has a grandson? Will he be willing to say something to him?

Aryakt wasn't in control of his thoughts anymore. The situation was very complicated for a reasonably strong (emotionally) person. For Aryakt, it was out of hands. He wanted to stay there and wished to talk to his grandfather, but at the same time, he tried to get to his daily routine and be alone comfortably.

While he fought this battle in his mind, he felt a movement on his hands. The thin, fleshless hand moved a little. He lifted his head immediately and shifted his sight from his hands to his face. Mrs. Gowri ran to the doctor to call him. Aryakt was left alone in the ICU with his grandfather. Mr. Srivatsa then blinked his eyes. Aryakt couldn't take his hands away from his grandfather's hand. It was comforting him. He observed the blink of his eyes and the hand movement again.

Meanwhile, Dr. Garg rushed into the ICU and monitored the pulse and blood pressure. It was alright. The doctor tried to talk to him by touching his shoulders.

"Your grandson is here - Aryakt," he said aloud.

The rate of eye blinking had increased. Mr. Srivatsa moved his head towards the doctor and looked into his eyes. He may have followed the direction of sound. The expression, though, was flat and weak. The doctor brought Aryakt to the front and took his name. Mr. Srivatsa looked at Aryakt plainly. The doctor patted Aryakt's shoulders and repeated his name.

"He is your grandson – Aryakt. Do you remember your grandson? Grandson!"

Mr. Srivatsa started to breathe heavily. The pulse rate was increasing. He was trying to lift his hand, but he couldn't. With increased efforts, he tried again unsuccessfully. He then tried to say something but couldn't. He started moving his eyes randomly, trying to focus on Aryakt.

"We should get him back to be calm. His nerves were conditioned to be calm for all these years. It's not good for him to put so much effort at once. Please be waited outside," the doctor said, looking at Aryakt.

As Aryakt started moving, Mr. Srivatsa made some sounds. Aryakt turned around, surprised. Randomly looking at everyone, Mr. Srivatsa indicated his stare towards Aryakt. Dr. Garg asked Aryakt to come near the bed. Mr. Srivatsa tried to smile, looking at Aryakt. He started breathing heavily and tried talking. He couldn't pronounce any word, but it was evident that he wished to speak to Aryakt.

Dr. Garg then forcibly took Aryakt out of the ICU. A couple of hours passed, and Mr. Srivatsa was still fully awake. Medication was given to control his medical parameters. Mr. Srivatsa has indicated his urge to talk to Aryakt. As he started uttering some words, the doctor and nurse felt surprised. The doctor allowed Mrs. Gowri to call Aryakt into the ICU.

Mr. Srivatsa then gestured for the doctor and nurse to leave the room. The doctor cautioned Aryakt not to talk about anything that could provoke his grandfather's emotional nerves.

A tense situation turned into a dreadful one for Aryakt. He held himself in control and got near his grandfather. Mr. Srivatsa looked at Aryakt with wide-open eyes. He called Aryakt to come near him and asked to sit beside him on the bed. Aryakt obliged to it hesitantly.

Mr. Srivatsa fought through his dried vocal cords and tried speaking. He said in a highly husky voice.

"I am your grandfather. Do you remember me?"

The first indication of someone related to Aryakt was humongous relief but an unusual one, given the circumstances.

Aryakt collected all his generosity and spoke. He said, "Yes. I do."

Then something weird happened. Mr. Srivatsa started laughing without making much sound. Aryakt was startled. That creepy laugh of his grandfather held some meaning in it. There was an aura of unusualness. It seemed like someone possessed him. A vibration of some big happening - could be good or bad. Aryakt could see the shrunk pupil of his grandfather's eyes expand. His eyes were getting brighter with every passing moment. He suddenly lifted his hand and placed it on Aryakt's palm. The weird sound of his laugh created discomfort in Aryakt, who was now afraid of his grandfather's behaviour. The airflow through his lungs might have made some void in his throat, so he stammered a lot while talking again. He said:

"I have something to......to..... to...."

Aryakt tried to figure out what he was trying to say. He said: "To give?"

Mr. Srivatsa nodded his head wildly in agreement.

"Bring my.....ba.....ba..." he stammered.

Aryakt asked, "Bag?"

A wild nod again. It made Aryakt feel insane.

Aryakt went out to talk to the nurse, and Mr. Srivatsa keenly looked at Aryakt's every movement. Aryakt was soon back with the bag.

With shivering hands, Mr. Srivatsa took the bag and randomly started searching through it. Finally, he took out a photograph from it. He couldn't hold it properly. There was no synchronisation between his fingers to get hold of the photograph. The desperation with which Mr. Srivatsa looked at Aryakt was highly uncomfortable, and Aryakt felt himself running out of the hospital at once.

"This is very imp..... imp...."

"Important," Aryakt helped.

The wild nod again.

"Listen to me carefully. There is a sec.... sec.... sec...."

"Second photograph?"

"Nooooo....... Maybe"

"There is a sec.... sec.... sec.... in...... in.... this photo"

Aryakt started uttering words with 'sec' – "Security, Secular, Secluded, Secret....."

Mr. Srivatsa stopped him abruptly, again nodding wildly as his hands shivered.

"Secret?"

"You mean, there is a secret in this photograph."

Mr. Srivatsa looked at Aryakt keenly. He seemed like his looks were trying to pierce through Aryakt's eyes and then to his mind.

He then said, "There is a tre... tre...tre..." and indicated something significant with his hands. His inclusiveness in the situation and those bright eyes made Aryakt feel panic.

"Train?"

"No. Tre.. Tre.." Mr. Srivatsa started moving his hands, indicating something huge again.

"Treasure?" Aryakt asked.

The wild nod again.

"Tre.... Tre.... If you crack the sec....sec...."

"You mean, I'll get a treasure if I can crack the secret in this photograph? Is that what you mean?"

Mr. Srivatsa started laughing aloud. Now, the extreme husky sound began to clear a little. Aryakt was in complete panic and got up from the bed at once. He looked around in confusion and shouted for the nurse and the doctor. The vehement look of his grandfather petrified Aryakt. The nurse rushed inside along with two ward boys.

Everyone was shocked to see the visual. Mr. Srivatsa was laughing aloud. The volume increased as the moments passed—more of a roar than amusement. The nurse and the ward boys tried to hold him and calm him. As Aryakt started moving out of the ICU, Mr. Srivatsa almost shouted, "Don't forget what I said. It is very imp...... imp..... imp.... for you."

As Aryakt got out and was almost closing the door of the ICU, he saw a sight that he could never forget in his lifetime. Mr. Srivatsa was patting his own shoulders wildly and laughing aloud. It clearly showed the sign of someone possessing his grandfather. It wasn't a bewilderment but a state of trance.

Door closed.

That jubilant laughter was still exploding in his ears as if he were seated next to his grandfather.

He ran towards the hospital exit and sat on a chair on the lawn. After around thirty minutes, Mrs. Gowri, the nurse, was at the reception and saw Aryakt. She called him in a hurry. With her head down, she said:

"I am very sorry to inform you of this. Your grandfather's pulse rate started dipping down uncontrollably, and probably it was a brain stroke. Mr. Srivatsa is no more." and continued,

"I couldn't imagine why his behaviour was so wild. Why was that wild laugh? What was he saying to you when you were with him? What's so important that he mentioned to you?" asked the nurse as Aryakt could only look at her keenly.

He then looked around randomly as if he was searching for his grandfather or probably for his ghost.

❑

Chapter 10

Aryakt telephoned Madhava and Sameer without a second thought while the nurse wrote the death notice of Mr. Srivatsa. Dr. Garg asked Aryakt about what his grandfather had told him before his death. Aryakt didn't answer it.

The only blood relative of his to whom he spoke just for five minutes was no more now—those five minutes weighed way beyond Aryakt's expectations. He wasn't an orphan all these years, and he always felt emotionally tied to his grandfather, even though they never spoke. He *is* indeed an orphan now.

At least for those five minutes, he felt the warmth as he touched his grandfather's hand. Now, as he thinks of it, it was the warmth that he never felt with anyone else. It was evident that his grandfather was concerned for Aryakt. He remembered Aryakt all the time.

Madhava and Sameer reached the hospital. Talking to Aryakt was a challenging task for them. From a distance, as they found Aryakt seated on the chair on the lawn, they found his loneliness heartbreaking. The friends ran to him and hugged him. Aryakt felt relieved at once, bringing tears to his eyes as he realised his loneliness.

Few people from the orphanage (where Aryakt spent his childhood) attended the funeral. Madhava and Sameer never left Aryakt alone during the day.

The three friends reached Aryakt's home in the evening. After spending some time, his friends unwillingly started to leave.

"Wait. How much did the whole thing cost?" asked Aryakt.

This expense is the one thing that Madhava wanted Aryakt to pay for. He calculated the costs and said, "It's twenty-five thousand rupees."

The number stuck Aryakt's mind like a shock. He got up and opened a tin box where he had placed the cash before getting it deposited into the bank account every month. There were around eight hundred rupees. Quickly, he searched for his bank passbook and hurriedly flipped its pages. On the last page, the entry says twenty-four thousand. Adding the cash in hand still wasn't enough to pay for the funeral of his grandfather. This was the money that his grandfather had left in his account. He has saved it for many years now.

Helpless, Aryakt sat on the cot and started crying. Madhava and Sameer tried to console him, but they couldn't.

"I am such a loser that I cannot even pay for the funeral of my grandfather."

"You can pay it later." Said Madhava.

"No. I should pay for it now. At least for the funeral." Aryakt said, quickly took his wallet, and started getting down the staircase. Sameer tried to stop him, but Madhava held Sameer's hand.

"Let him go. He is going to withdraw cash. Let him go. The anguish is what is needed to change his thought process."

After an hour, Aryakt was back with twenty thousand rupees.

"I am not allowed to withdraw more than twenty thousand in a day. I'll give the remaining money tomorrow."

"Well, okay. How do you know that twenty thousand is the maximum withdrawal limit in a day?" asked Madhava keenly.

Sameer understood the purpose of the question and nodded.

"I couldn't draw more than that. The machine said the maximum limit was reached. And then I asked the security guard of the ATM and got the same answer."

Madhava looked at Sameer and smiled. He said, "Okay. Never mind, give the remaining money tomorrow."

The two friends got out of the house after a while.

"Finally, he spoke to some unknown person willingly," Sameer said.

"Of course, Sameer. I always think the solution to Aryakt's problem lies in his adversity. Those adverse situations will either break him or make him break the records, which he is always capable of. Do you remember him teaching us our nightmare subjects during school? I used to get inspired by him. The way he thought about the problems and solved them." Madhava said and walked in silence for a minute.

Sameer looked at him and said, "Now he is left with nothing as his savings. And he never borrows money from us. What will he do? These tuition fees will not earn him much money, and I doubt he demands timely fees from those kids."

Madhava took a couple of cigarettes from his pocket and gave one to Sameer. Both looked at each other and decided to keep those cigarettes in their pocket. A sense of disappointment was in the air.

"He needs some miracle to happen," Sameer said, looking at the penthouse as they walked on the road.

"And *he* needs to create it," Madhava said, looking at the sky as he felt helpless.

Even though the friends always wanted to help Aryakt in all the ways possible, Aryakt never asked for any help from them, and neither did he took it when offered. Madhava took out the cigarette box and threw it into the dustbin. He tried to control his helplessness, which built a little frustration in him.

"Let us hope some miracle would happen," Madhava said, getting into his car.

"Soon," Sameer completed the sentence.

The days passed by, and Aryakt's financial crisis increased in a big way. He last paid his house rent three months ago. He got the awaited blood tests, and the reports came out normal. His earnings out of tuition were just sufficient for his basic needs. Aryakt started skipping his dinner to save some money. One fine day, when he drank five glasses of water for dinner, he sat on the terrace looking at the sky. Suddenly, the words of his grandfather flashed in his mind.

He remembered the nurse giving him the bag with all his grandfather's belongings. He brought the bag and sat on the terrace. The full moonlight illuminated the bag that was torn in some places. There was a spectacle, a lighter, comb, shirt and trousers. The shirt pocket had *that* photograph that his grandfather had shown him.

Aryakt looked at it keenly. It was a photograph of three old men, probably friends. They had their hands on each other's shoulders, and all three were ecstatic. It was during sunset (or sunrise) at a beach. The wavy seashore was well visible. The white stripes of waves cutting through the infinite blue sea made the background perfect for a photograph. The friends were enjoying the time to the fullest.

Aryakt rushed into the room and observed the photograph under the light. The person standing in the middle resembled his grandfather. Aryakt cleared his eyes and keenly observed that person's face. Yes, he indeed was his grandfather, Mr. Srivatsa.

He looked younger than he was in the ICU. Yet he looked around sixty years of age in the photograph. Aryakt recollected that the death notice mentioned that his grandfather was eighty-four years old when he died. For the last twenty-two years, he has been in a coma. The photograph should have been at least twenty-two years old. So, he should be at most sixty-two when this picture was captured.

The other two people were almost the same age. The photograph was well-protected and didn't have many stains on it. He flipped it and saw the mention of the date December 8. Aryakt thought for a while about what secret the photograph had in it.

❑

Chapter 11

The days passed by, and Aryakt started feeling embarrassed by his situation. At times, he thought about Sheela Aunty. Even though her presence during the party made him uneasy, she always tried to engage him in some activity. The name 'activity' created less panic in him these days, that is, after that party. Thanks to Sheela Aunty.

Aryakt had to repay the money to Madhava as soon as possible. Although Madhava didn't mention it anytime, Aryakt felt a virtual pressure. There indeed was a need, he felt, to ramp up his income through some means other than teaching. The means should not involve talking to people.

He met the local newspaper distributor in-charge, and by accumulating tremendous courage, he asked him if he could allot Aryakt some localities to deliver the newspapers. The in-charge then demanded some money to be deposited. Even though the money was small, Aryakt couldn't afford it.

Much likely because of Aryakt's state of mind, he looked restless, and his eyes looked tired. The in-charge understood it the other way. As Aryakt started leaving the place, the in-charge said, looking at the person seated beside him, "These young drug addicts do not want to spend money on good things."

Aryakt held his panic behind the "so-called" confident gesture, but that comment broke him. His eyes unknowingly were pouring out tears. He couldn't run to his home because the people around *would* focus on a person randomly running on the main road. He just walked crying with his head down, ensuring no one could see his tears.

Sameer and Madhava were waiting for Aryakt on the terrace as he reached the room. He looked dreadful with red eyes. Aryakt hugged Sameer and cried aloud. Madhava took the cigarette pack from his pocket and started flipping it with his fingers. He observed Aryakt keenly.

Getting into the home, Aryakt explained what had happened. Sameer felt sad for Aryakt and asked, "Why are you so worried about the money you owe Maddy? You can return it later."

"Later, when? After I die?" Aryakt replied in frustration.

"No Aryakt. Don't be so upset. Do you want to work in Madhava's startup company? I am sure he'll have some job for you." Sameer said and looked at Madhava, who was still looking at Aryakt keenly.

"Maddy?!...... Say something." Sameer shouted.

Madhava got back to his senses and nodded his head.

"See. You can work in Madhava's company."

Hearing the words 'job in a company' made Aryakt afraid and panicked again. *I'll have to talk to people. I'll have to answer people. I'll have to be with people.*

"No. No. No. No job. Please, No job." Aryakt started walking swiftly inside the room.

Madhava stopped flipping the cigarette pack and threw it into the dustbin disappointingly.

Madhava said, "Look, Aryakt. If you do not want to work in a company, you can very well....". The knock on the door made Madhava abruptly stop his sentence.

It was the house owner of the building, in which Aryakt was one of the tenants. Aryakt set himself well and looked surprised to see the house owner at his doorstep for the first time in years. The house owner was well-dressed and well-behaved.

"I am sorry to have bothered you." He said, sitting on the cot as the three friends stood before him.

He looked at them, smiled hesitantly, and said, "I don't even remember the last time when I spoke to this person. It was when he and some of his colleagues from an orphanage were here looking for a rented house for him. And now I am in front of him again talking," he said and continued,

"Every month, he comes to our home downstairs on the ground floor, pays the rent in cash, and calmly leaves. I never got a chance to speak to him. I know from the kids - his students that he does not like to talk to anyone. Well, then, I understood his situation and never bothered him. Aryakt is your name. Right!" he stopped for a moment for Aryakt's nod and continued.

"But now I had to come here to inform you about one of my needs. Please do not take it otherwise. My son is getting married two months from now. We want to use this penthouse ourselves. So, if you can look for a house elsewhere and vacate the penthouse, I'll be thankful."

As the friends looked questioningly and Aryakt was almost about to burst out into tears again, the house owner took a leave after he said, "Thank you. And I am sorry to have halted your discussion. Think and let me know, please."

Sameer held his head with his two hands. Madhava again looked keenly at Aryakt, seated on the floor, staring at his lap.

He didn't speak when Sameer asked what he wanted to do next. Instead, he lifted his head, saw the ceiling, and closed his eyes.

Madhava stopped Sameer, disturbing Aryakt. Aryakt opened his eyes wide after around five minutes. He got up, took a book from the neatly maintained shelves, and swiftly descended the stairs. Sameer and Madhava ran behind him to see what he was up to.

Sameer tried to stop Aryakt, who was walking swiftly on the footpath. Aryakt turned around, said, "For God's sake, leave me alone," and walked away.

Madhava stopped Sameer and said, "Come here with me."

Madhava bought a pack of cigarettes, took one, and offered one to Sameer. Sameer took his electric lighter from his pocket. Madhava asked him to keep it back. He then took the matchbox from the shopkeeper and lit both cigarettes.

Taking a deep puff, and as the smoky exhale filled the air around Sameer's face, Madhava said, "This is the *real* fire. Not your electric lighter."

Sameer looked at Madhava questioningly as his eyes got smaller. He then realised something, looked around, and saw Aryakt walking swiftly, probably unsure of where he was going.

Sameer turned towards Madhava and asked, "Adversity?"

Madhava nodded.

Sameer thought for a while, saying, "One shouldn't bite off more than he can chew. It's hard for him, I guess. We are expecting too much from Aryakt here."

Madhava nodded his head and said, "No. Don't say that. It isn't too much at all. Believe me. Records should break now."

❑

Chapter 12

With a bent head, Aryakt walked without a halt for four long hours that didn't seem so long. Multiple thoughts popped up in his mind and jumped around without his conscious effort. He didn't try to control or bring thoughts into a specific pattern. He just walked and walked. His emotional conscience wasn't tired yet, but his physical tiredness started sending signals to his brain. He fought them away for another thirty minutes and slowly brought himself to a halt.

As he moved his head up, unsure after how much time, he felt an extreme pain in the back of his neck. But the sight in front of him created an ecstatic feeling. The greenery around without the sight of a human being was blissful. The sky wasn't visible much as the dark clouds masked it.

He saw very few vehicles passing through but at very high speeds. He figured out that he had touched a highway at some side of the outskirts of Vizag. He wasn't sure about the time of the day, but it seemed around afternoon.

He then tried to bring his popping thoughts under control as he chose a tree away from the road and sat under it. He ignored the feeling of thirst since he saw no place around him where he could purchase a water bottle. As he got into the dense green trees, he observed a flower that was deep inside a tree. It was yellowish and had glowing orange patches on its sepal. His thoughts went around that flower, and he murmured to himself. *Why is this beautiful flower blossoming here? Who will see it? No one. Who will appreciate its beauty and the courage to grow inside these dense leaves?*

He then suggested to himself: *It should have been a wildflower. Inevitable to take birth.*

In contrast, he thought: *What if it took birth for a purpose?*

He then moved forward and looked at the book that he held. Looking at the book cover in his hand and noticing the oddly written name of aNoNyMoUs, he smiled a little.

He had already completed reading around half of the book, and he didn't have much of a need to search for that small paper marking fold. He knew where to resume. Lying on the trunk of a big neem tree, he immersed himself in the book. The instances portrayed in the book were what he always faced in his life. *Are there other people in this world who were/are as introverted as me? How would they lead their lives in this outspoken, extrovert world?* He thought.

It started breezing a little, and without anyone around, Aryakt felt the atmosphere becoming cosy. The book gave multiple instances of motivating an introvert to socialise. As he reached the last page, he read something that moved him. It said:

If you can do something good, then the biggest crime you can commit is not doing that good. Life is all about knowing and doing 'that' good which you can do.

The book ended with a sentence: *A commoner's anguish does not harm the world to the extent that the silence of a genius does.*

Aryakt was left heavy in his thoughts, but then he thought the world was not as lovely as the author thought. *The world is not so dependent on an individual*, either. The cold breeze increased its speed. The nimbostratus clouds filled the sky, and the sun that was hidden somewhere behind them didn't have any impact whatsoever. It seemed that it was going to rain heavily. Aryakt ran across a giant tree beside the main road and stood under it. After around two minutes, it started raining heavily. He tried to fit the book in his pocket, protecting it from the rain. Once he accomplished it, he felt the hunger that had been there for a long time but emerged as he stopped *thinking*.

As it started pouring, he saw an old man run under the same tree and stood beside him. He was tall and lean. His white beard and white hair seemed to have been trimmed a very long time ago. His attire made him look dreadful, and he was penniless. The old man carried a big plastic sheet on his head. It covered his entire body. It made a triangle shape around him, and Aryakt started looking away from him, squeezing his palms. He was not so afraid of staying beside kids or older people. So, he wasn't anxious, at least.

The old man started shivering after some time. The freezing breeze pinched every part of Aryakt's skin, and he, too, started shivering with cold. No other thought he had now - only the cool breeze and the feeling of his bones dancing inside his body and those unmoved muscles that needed some heat.

The old man looked at Aryakt and offered him his plastic raincoat. Aryakt couldn't reject it and took it at once. He wore it and squeezed his body to immerse in that 'so-called' raincoat. The old man wrapped his hands around Aryakt to give him a little warmth as he shivered more.

Aryakt looked at him from inside the raincoat and felt amazed at the view. The old man shivered so much but still rubbed Aryakt's body to create some heat. Aryakt felt safe inside that oversized raincoat even though a completely unknown man stood so close beside him. After around thirty minutes, the rain stopped, and Aryakt's guilt of capturing the raincoat from that old man immediately showed up. He came out of it and returned it to the old man.

He laughed aloud, saying, "What do I do with it now? The rain has stopped."

Aryakt said, "I am... I am sorry. I couldn't say no when you offered it."

"No problem. Well, you take this. And you look starving." The old man said, taking a piece of bread from his pocket.

The bread was broken into pieces. He segregated them into his hands and offered them to Aryakt. Aryakt hesitated and asked, "Are you not feeling cold?"

"I am," the old man said.

"Are you not hungry?"

"I am."

"Then why did you give me your raincoat? And why are you offering this bread to me?"

"I gave it because *you* were shivering. And I know by your face that you are starving."

"Do you have any more food for you?" Aryakt asked, shell-shocked.

"Nope," the old man said confidently.

Aryakt looked at him in surprise and just stayed silent.

"I'll have to go now. Thanks," the old man said.

As he moved away, Aryakt asked, "What do you do?"

"Now I do nothing" he replied, turning back.

As the old man walked further, Aryakt said aloud, "Why did you offer me your raincoat and food when you didn't have anything for yourself?"

The old man started walking swiftly and replied, "I feel hungry every day, and I shiver to the breeze every day."

Aryakt stayed silent as the old man walked away from him and turned toward the other side of the road. The old man shouted, "If you can do something good and aren't, then it's a crime. You know!" He laughed aloud, "Haaa hahaha...Haaa hahah."

Aryakt's thought froze for a second as he heard the diminishing sound of the old man's voice. The laugh vibrated in his ears, holding a firm and authentic pitch. The thing the old man said was almost the same as stated in that book. Setting right his hair, Aryakt ran across to find the old man. As he turned towards the way the old man had walked, there was no one.

"Who was he?" Aryakt asked himself.

He ate the bread, which couldn't fulfil his hunger but was enough to deceive his brain of the extreme hunger. He then folded the raincoat, held it in his hand, and started walking back home.

He couldn't control his surprise when he again realised that the old man was hungry and shivering from the cold breeze every day.

He didn't have any need to offer the raincoat or the food. But still, he did, like 'that' blossoming flower which will surely go unnoticed by anyone. The old man represented that flower. It didn't go unnoticed, and that old man shouldn't go unnoticed. Who should notice him? Me. He represented the niceness of this world like that flower. He represented the person that aNoNyMoUs said about in his book.

Was he the aNoNyMoUs?

Aryakt controlled his tears, held the raincoat firmly, and started running towards the beautiful and ever-inviting city of Vizag.

❑

Chapter 13

The whole night went by uneasily for Aryakt, and the thoughts of that old man and the flower weren't getting out of his mind. There wasn't a relation between the two. But Aryakt had it in perfect synchronisation for him. He never could disconnect them.

He felt relieved as he saw the early morning sun with his students at home on time. Relieved nerves. The students could make out that Aryakt wasn't in his usual manner.

They wished him as usual. After wishing them back, Aryakt entered the washroom as the kids sat on the carpet sequentially. Aryakt washed his face, and as he looked into the mirror, a sight flashed in his mind, making him rattle.

Setting himself right, he joined the kids. He looked at Mugdha, who was taking out her mathematics textbook, probably to clear some of her doubts in calculus. Aryakt was hesitant. He never thought he'd be uncertain of his students, whom he loved wholeheartedly.

"Mugdha, were you in that engagement function of Madhava's cousin?"

Mugdha looked at him, startled. Pondering about how and when Aryakt would have noticed her, she nodded.

Aryakt's heart started pacing. He was at the zenith of his disturbance.

"Were you dancing anytime at that function?"

Mugdha understood about when Aryakt had noticed her. She nodded again.

Aryakt sat in silence, wondering and probably worrying. *For what? Still trying to figure it out.* He understood something about himself yet again. Why was he afraid that Mugdha was dancing at a party? Does he want her to be like him? An introvert. No. But still, he felt uncomfortable. Probably because he never saw her like that. He spoke to himself that she was a grown-up girl now. She'll have her aspirations. She would want to turn moments into memories. She is no longer a small girl to whom he started teaching mathematics when she was in second grade. Aryakt started realising the well-read theory of 'Change is the only constant.' He also understood that life keeps proving theories, but the right vision is needed to realise it.

Aryakt looked at Mugdha and smiled hesitantly. His smile had unknowingly broken one of his impenetrable and incorrect perceptions.

As the kids left after an hour, Aryakt cooked his breakfast and ate it.

He started thinking about his following accomplishments of the day. The laugh of that old man had built some confidence in him. As he looked at the calendar hung on the wall, the two-month notice was the first thing to hit his mind.

He either will have a dreadful time going further, which will be in his comfort zone, or he'll have to come out of that comfort and take on a tiring, fearful, uneasy, and random journey. He knew what he had to do. He sat in peace on the terrace and meditated. He felt all his senses aiding his decision. The only thing that was opposing it was his mind. It wants him to live in his comfort zone. He recollected the old man's laugh and the flower's blossom. It triggered some smile in him. Still, the mind wasn't ready to flow with his decision. He then recollected the problems he had. Not financial, but emotional. He remembered the way he lived his life so far. Those anxious moments he had when he walked on the crowded roads. The dreadful feeling that he had when a group of youngsters passed by him on the road. The sweaty forehead he had every day whenever he saw someone and anticipated that he had to talk to that person. The increase in the pace of the heartbeat when someone laughs for some reason, and he assumes that the laugh is to mock him and make fun of him.

The nervous feeling when he thinks about his mother and tries to imagine how she would have dealt with his problem. The extreme nervousness that he felt while realising that he mostly imagined his mother but ignored his father. He imagined his father's smiling face and the comfort he would have given him during every challenging moment. Had his parents been alive today, then he would have been a better person with *some* confidence, at least.

His mind again tried to get him out of the meditation by creating fear. Gathering together the happiness of the unrealised feeling of sleeping in his mother's lap, the unrealised confidence of sitting in front of his father while he drove the motorcycle, the unrealised relief with his grandfather holding his hand and comforting him for his introverted behaviour, saying – 'It'll be alright, but it'll take some time, I am here with you.', Aryakt brought himself close to a decision.

He then recollected the final words of the book. He thought, *I am not a genius, and the sentence doesn't apply to me. But..... But what if I am?*

He spoke some conclusive words to himself. His words came out stammering as he made his life's most significant decision.

I'll not bother about my anxiety for the people around me. After all, I am one of them. I am not inferior to them. I am just anybody from the crowd. I'll have to find the truth behind the secret treasure. If I am destined to find the treasure, I'll have to give my part to discover it. My grandfather wanted me to get to it.

I'll get to it. The journey would be challenging. It was an impossible task till yesterday. But not now. If a flower can, an old man can, and a book can, then why can't I?

Yes, I can.

I know where to start.

❑

Chapter 14

Aryakt anticipated a journey. A journey to find the secret behind the mysterious photograph. A journey that was capable of imploding his very being. Placing the photograph inside the book he read the previous day, he locked the penthouse door and started.

He opted to walk to the orphanage and reached at around 4 PM. A forgotten fragrance resurrected itself, leaving him in thoughts for a few minutes. Standing in front of the orphanage's main gate, he, with great fondness, recollected the childhood days that he had spent in it. Without the orphanage's care, his life would have been a misery. For many, it wasn't only the shelter but also the temple of discipline. It gave him all the basic needs and, more importantly, the chance and access to education.

One person who had served thousands of kids for many years and had spent most of her life serving in the same orphanage was Miss Sudha. Aryakt waited for her in the temple inside the orphanage. After fifteen minutes, Miss Sudha entered the temple with a pleasant face and a peaceful smile. She always was very conservative and sweet in her words. Her accommodative nature made the kids feel a motherly comfort with her.

She looked at Aryakt, smiling. She remembered him well because he grew up mostly in her care. Being one of those rare kids with extreme intelligence and extreme anxiousness, Aryakt's presence was always felt by her. Even though conceding that Aryakt had a big problem, Miss Sudha had never given up. The little confidence that Aryakt had was because of her. She greeted him with a smile.

Deliberately getting into a fluster was Aryakt's expertise, and when the matter is about a discussion, then it ought to emerge. Sweat started popping up all over his forehead, not because of Miss Sudha but because of the topic he wanted to discuss with her. His senses forced him to run away from the orphanage, but he tried to keep his mind in control. He murmured the piezoelectric effect to restráin his panic, and as Miss Sudha moved forward towards him, he swallowed the Hall effect, which he thought to murmur next.

"Great to see you, Aryakt. How are you?" Miss Sudha asked, observing the sweat on his forehead.

"I am good, Miss Sudha," Aryakt said unconfidently.

"Good. Do you want to talk to me regarding something?" she asked, trying to bring him to the point. She knew that keeping Aryakt 'to the point' was the best thing to do while he was in a panic.

"Yes"

"Then tell me. What do you want to talk about?" Miss Sudha said, still maintaining the smile on her face.

Aryakt inhaled a deep breath and turned around towards the idol of Lord Krishna. Miss Sudha walked to the other side and stood facing him. She said, "Do not worry. Tell me whatever you have in mind."

Aryakt looked into her eyes. Those eyes always held compassion for everyone. Probably, they reflected her state of mind. *Yes, eyes do reflect that*. The following deep exhaling breath took out most of his negative thoughts as he recollected the moments, he spent talking with her, which relieved him. He said at once, which surprised Miss Sudha.

"I would like to know the details of the person who admitted me into this orphanage."

She raised her eyebrows, thought momentarily, and said, "It was your grandfather, Mr. Srivatsa." She stopped for a moment and continued, "I feel sad that your only blood relative, your grandfather, is no more. Even though he wasn't with you physically anytime, he was your only family member whom I know."

Aryakt just stared at the ground. Miss Sudha instantly recollected something. She hurriedly said, "Another person, probably his friend, has accompanied him. Yes, he indeed was his friend. I remember Mr. Srivatsa mentioning that. I think he was the witness during your admission here."

Aryakt felt daunted listening to those words, 'friend of your grandfather.' He held Miss Sudha's hand and asked, "Do you remember who that person was? I mean, his name."

Miss Sudha thought for a moment and said, "It was very long ago. I do not remember his name off hand."

Aryakt held her palm tight and asked, "Can you remember his face?"

"I am not sure I do."

Aryakt opened his bag and took out the photograph from the book. Showing it to Miss Sudha, he asked excitedly as panic disappeared.

"Is it anyone from these two?"

Miss Sudha could recognise Mr. Srivatsa, and she observed the faces of the other two men keenly. She said irresolutely,

"Maybe this person. I can't remember exactly. But I think I saw this person."

It was the person standing on the extreme left. His hair was grey and around the same age as Mr. Srivatsa's.

"Are you sure?" he asked.

"No. But I think I saw this person. Where did you get this photograph from?"

"I.... I got it....." he hesitantly continued, "Miss Sudha, my grandfather gave me this photograph."

She looked at him in surprise and asked, "Why do you want to know about your grandfather's friend?"

Aryakt stayed silent.

"Alright. Come with me. We'll go through the records," she said, pulling Aryakt's hands with her.

Aryakt did not move. He said, "I am fine here, please."

"There is no one in my office room. You needn't talk to anyone," Miss Sudha said understandingly.

"I am okay here, please," he requested.

Miss Sudha nodded and swiftly walked out of the temple. Aryakt waited patiently, but his heartbeat started ramping as time passed.

After around fifteen minutes, Miss Sudha was back with a register.

"Here it is." She showed the opened register where there was a pencil mark.

"He was the witness, yes. His name is Mohan R. Here is his address."

The address mentioned was of Perambra in Calicut, Kerala state. Aryakt could hear his next heartbeat quite clearly. It was like an explosion of fear inside him. His mind couldn't take in that he'd have to go to Kerala, probably alone, as he didn't want to disturb his friends or seek any more help from them.

He wished to go out as soon as he could. Loneliness was his unparalleled acquaintance.

"Can I note this address?"

"Yes, of course."

Aryakt noted it in his extraordinary handwriting, undeteriorated even in his disquiet state of mind.

He thanked Miss Sudha and left the orphanage. Looking at Aryakt as he left, Miss Sudha felt happy.

"Good for him," she thought.

❑

Chapter 15

Seated on the lawn behind the orphanage building, Aryakt read the address around twenty times, yet the word 'Kerala' had the same feeling every time he uttered it. He had never gone anywhere out of Vizag. His mind was forcing him to withdraw from the mission. The house owner's words flashed in his mind, and the mission became inevitable. Motivation was there, but the implementation – was it easy for him? No. Not at all.

He took a piece of paper and a pen from the bag and forcibly started writing down the list of things he needed to prepare before he could kick off the mission.

Stop being afraid of people around you.

Start travelling by bus/auto-rickshaw/train.

Dare to talk to a stranger.

Look into the eyes of the person you are talking to.

Loneliness is not your friend.

Arrange some money – discovering the secret isn't a cheap affair.

He read the points many times to cement them in his mind, though implementing these would demand his blood and sweat.

As he packed his bag with a sigh of forcible relief and as a start, he planned to take an auto-rickshaw home.

There were many of them waiting for the passengers. Aryakt got near one of them and asked for Seetamma dhaara.

"Yes. Sit inside towards the extreme right," the driver, standing leaning toward the auto-rickshaw, said in a loud voice. He then started shouting the names of other nearby locations around Seetamma dhaara.

A lady then got into it and sat beside Aryakt. She looked around thirty-five. Aryakt sat leaning on Pawan Kalyan's photo on his right. Even though he closed his eyes to control the panic of being seated beside a lady, his forehead started sweating heavily.

Another man around forty-five came in, and the driver started the engine. That man sat beside the driver. As the driver changed the gear, another lady of around fifty years got in and sat beside the other. Aryakt almost got squeezed and turned his head towards the right to look away from the lady beside him. Pawan Kalyan was right in front of his eyes, holding a shotgun.

The auto-rickshaw just started, and another lady stopped it.

"Get in, madam. Get in soon," the driver said.

Get in? Where? As the lady beside him started to move, squeezing him a little more, Aryakt felt breathless and exited the auto-rickshaw from his side, jumping above the metallic fence at the right-side exit. To escape the discussion with the auto-driver, he ran in the other direction without looking back.

The lady beside him was flabbergasted and immediately checked her belongings in the handbag, fearing Aryakt to be a thief. She felt relieved that everything in it was intact.

The driver laughed aloud and moved ahead, murmuring something, probably some abusive words.

Aryakt then walked to his home, as usual.

By the evening, when he started getting irritated with his mindset, he walked to the nearest library. The best thing with the library, he felt, was the mention of 'Silence, please.' No one would talk to him. Even if they were observing him, they wouldn't speak.

He searched the entire library and found an old copy of a book by 'aNoNyMoUs.' It was the book released before the one which he read already. He spent many hours in the library reading. At closing time, the librarian allowed Aryakt to take that book home even though he didn't have a membership card. The librarian believed him since he had seen Aryakt many times and knew him by face.

The only motivation that Aryakt could get was from a book. This book he picked up induced a stream of thought-provoking ideas. His intent to change himself was rigid in its place.

Aryakt thought there was a need to be harsh to himself now. He should be hard on his comforts. He took an auto-rickshaw to the library again the next day to return the book. He returned home in a city bus – one of his biggest nightmares. Even though the unrest had shown up on his face, he could make the trip successful.

The 'secret treasure' was on his mind all the time. He tried changing his daily routine and included 'people' around him. Though unconfidently, he spoke to people. The sweat on his forehead, representing his panic, still had shown up at times. He even had some panic attacks with breathlessness that he started controlling successfully.

His confidence was showing up to his students as well. The fear of being in anxiety trembles a man more than the anxiety itself. Aryakt started to realise it.

Aryakt's subconscious was confident, but his conscious mind wasn't yet. It still needed some grooming. As he got used to travelling by public transport and started talking to people, he decided that it was time for the Odyssey.

❑

Chapter 16

Let Me Take It Alone

The clock ticked 8 PM when Aryakt sat on the terrace after having dinner. Being alone wasn't a pain, but it pinched him a little that day. He ignored it and murmured to himself, which made him comfortable.

If this person in the photograph is Mohan R, then I should be able to know my grandfather's life. I know that he worked in the army for some time. Nothing else. If Mohan R accompanied my grandfather during my admission to the orphanage, then he should have been a very good friend of my grandfather. It is obvious that the three friends in this photograph were on an excursion, and Mohan R is one of them (hopefully, as Miss Sudha couldn't recognise him confidently). If I believe that Mohan R was one of those two friends whose address I know, then the first thing to start with is to meet Mohan R.

Two questions arise. One - Is Mohan R still alive? Two - Is he residing at the same place mentioned in the orphanage records? There was no mention of the telephone number. I should check if he is still alive and living at that address.

As her got up from the chair, something had struck his thought. He felt his next heartbeat skip. A question that was so obvious to be asked. *Why did my grandfather admit me into an orphanage himself? All these years, I thought I got into the orphanage after he met with an accident. I was wrong. Why did he admit me while he was well? Was he anticipating this accident? Was his life in danger? I should take this up for him, at least.*

The word 'Kerala' again triggered some panic, but he swallowed it. After packing the necessary things to survive for at least a week, Aryakt telephoned Mugdha's home landline. Mugdha's mother took it. After wishing her well, Aryakt asked for Mugdha.

"Hello, Mugdha. I'll not be available for the next week at home. So, please continue on your own. Advanced composite mathematics is where you need some practice. Visualise things, and then you'll understand it. Also, please inform the other kids. I have the syllabus covered for them almost. So, needn't worry for them."

Mugdha was surprised for quite a few reasons. Aryakt calling her over the telephone was the prime one of it. He is away from home for a week. *Where is he going?* Confidence in his voice. And lastly, with whom will he be for the entire week? *Is he going somewhere with Sameer and Madhava?*

Mugdha couldn't ask all these questions over the phone. Instead, she said, "Please take care, sir."

Mugdha felt worried about Aryakt. The kids loved their teacher from the core of their hearts. She considered ringing up one of his friends but decided against it since she never knew Aryakt's plan.

The following day, she got ready on time and reached Aryakt's home by 6 AM, hoping for Aryakt to be there. The other kids joined her. The penthouse was locked. They searched for their teacher around. None was on the terrace. They went to the house owner's residence on the ground floor—no information regarding Aryakt. The sad student group had dispersed to their respective homes.

Mugdha's anxiety was peaking up for her teacher, and finally, she called Madhava immediately after reaching her home. She explained her conversation with Aryakt to Madhava. He was surprised to hear it.

"One week. You mean, seven days? I don't know anything about it. I am sure Sameer wouldn't know either. Otherwise, he would have told me. Anyway, thanks a lot for letting me know this, Mugdha." Madhava said and disconnected the call.

Madhava called Sameer only to be disappointed that he didn't know where Aryakt had gone. Both friends reached Aryakt's home, and nothing was known about his whereabouts. They tried calling him over the phone, but the call went unanswered.

Sameer, seated on the terrace floor, said, "Now, where is this guy? I am afraid he is in some problem."

Madhava looked at him, tensed, and his phone then vibrated. It was Aryakt's message. It read: "I am out of station for some days. I am sorry for not informing you regarding the plan. Already, I owe you a lot of time and effort. I do not want to owe any more of those parameters. But finance isn't one of them. Could you please spare five thousand for me? You don't want to know when I will return it. But *I* do. And the answer is that *I don't know*. As I get on a mission, I hope to accomplish it without *your* efforts. My hope will hopefully be fulfilled. Meet you on the other side. I wish *you* to be with me. But I also wish you *not* to be with me."

Madhava raised his head and saw Sameer reading through something on his phone. It was the same message.

"Mission?!!!" Sameer exclaimed, getting up from the floor.

A questioning expression was on their faces. The first thing they did was to send Aryakt the money.

"Send him exactly five thousand. Don't send more. Otherwise, he will change his mission to return this additional money. ASAP." said Madhava.

Sameer laughed to himself, and both sent five thousand each. Sameer messaged Aryakt, saying:

"Sent. Why are you not taking the call? And what's this *mission*?"

Aryakt replied: "Thank you. Let me take it alone."

Aryakt replaced his phone in the pocket of his cotton trousers. The speed of Vivek Express increased as it left the platform, and so did Aryakt's heartbeat.

❑

Chapter 17

Though an alternative to the accepted 'Big Bang,' the oscillating universe has merits. The contraction and expansion of the universe and the hot, dense material eventually expanding and making a brighter sense of the matter is accepted, though not wholly. That seems a great explanation connecting them to the thoughts many intellectuals possess.

Even though the process of charge movements in a PN junction diode is due to the drift of electrons, the reason for current is still the process of diffusion since the electrons *diffuse* through the junction.

By the way, as the thoughts revolve around diffusion, the mind goes to the evolution of humankind, which is an infinite topic of study. Do we correlate the 'Mankind' with 'Life' since the ever-existing 'Life' doesn't necessarily wander only around 'Mankind'? However, if the so-called human is considered a subset of animals, the discussion converges, and the argument ends for a good and needed cause.

The upper berth was just enough for Aryakt not to get his feet out of the berth. Squeezing himself, he didn't try to hold his mind in a cage. It was wandering as it wished. Even though hungry, he felt comforted since he didn't have to talk to anyone, look at anyone, or participate in any discussion. He smiled as the water bottle carrier was in front of his eyes, hanging along the wall that divided two sections in the train. He closed his eyes as he thought about how the chess board could be designed for three players.

The Vivek Express reached the Kozhikode platform early in the morning, around 5 AM. With a small bag on the back and a protected mysterious photograph, Aryakt started walking swiftly out of the railway station. Taking out a paper from his bag, he looked around. He has all the detailed landmarks, routes, and shops along the road from Kozhikode railway station to Perambra bus stand written clearly on it.

How will he reach Mohan's home from the Perambra bus stand?

After walking around two kilometres uneasily, he felt the well-known excitement in him – walking. Without a second thought, he decided to walk to Perambra. He wasn't surprised at his decision. The decision to walk around forty kilometres made him realise that he was famished. His mindset of walking alone on the road without anyone's focus on him made him more tolerant of hunger.

After some unknown time, as the sunshine slowly pierced through the dense clouds into his eyes, he lifted his head to look around. The Perambra town was lively with people. The city wakes up early in the morning. The kids walked along the footpath with their school bags and little lunch boxes. The snack centres were crowded with people having their breakfast. Aryakt felt an increased hunger. But his panic was showing up in sweat on his forehead as he looked at the crowd in the snack centre.

What do I ask for? Idli? Dosa? How much would it cost? I should have practiced having some snacks away from home while being at Vizag.

"Where do you want to go?" a sound resounded in Aryakt's ears as an auto-rickshaw stood beside him, and the driver bent himself almost to a right angle.

Shocked by the sound, Aryakt jumped at once and turned around. The auto-rickshaw driver was utterly black with a fat face. He looked half tidy. Aryakt almost always believed that the auto-rickshaw drivers took advantage of innocent people. Immediately, without another thought, he replied, hiding his panic:

"Nowhere. I am just.... Just walking. It's not far.... My place. I am a local person."

"Alright," the driver moved ahead.

Aryakt moved ahead, raising his eyebrows and exhaling, acknowledging his escape from the driver.

Crossing the tiny road, he entered the main road where he was to see the bigger audience as if they were waiting to disturb his peace of mind.

A man who was equally black as the auto-rickshaw driver but relatively younger stood leaning against the wall of a meat store and looked at Aryakt. His muscles were showing up out of his half-shirt that was as untidy as the person's face. The person approached Aryakt and asked, "Do you want an auto-rickshaw or a cab? Or are you looking for any address?"

As he approached, a sharp adrenaline spiked in Aryakt. He, at once, took a couple of steps back and said, "No, no. Stay where you are."

The water bottle made of glass that was in Aryakt's hand fell on the ground and broke into pieces. The people around looked at Aryakt. He couldn't carry the focus of so many people at once. He closed his eyes tight.

"Alright. Alright. You look new to the place. So, I asked," the muscle man said.

"No. I am local to this place," Aryakt replied with his eyes still closed.

The street cleaners were on duty and started cleaning the broken pieces. Aryakt exhaled and moved forward swiftly as the muscle man got back and leaned against the same wall.

Upon taking some steps, he saw an old man holding a white bag standing in front of Aryakt, showing him a packet of vastra mala, and asked in his shaking pale voice: "Do you want to buy this? It is just ten rupees."

Aryakt took a few steps back and made a face, looking at the old man. But then, the old man retarded away from Aryakt.

Before Aryakt could get away from this unrest of people approaching him, a group of school children crossing the road made the traffic-jammed, and vehicles honked in desynchronization. Aryakt felt his head explode with the surrounding noise. He ran along about twenty steps and stood immobile to control himself.

❑

Chapter 18

As his thoughts reflected in him while he fought his panic and felt angry at himself for being so reluctant to people around, he heard the temple bells ring. He turned around to see that he was in front of a temple. The Lord Shiva seated in peace is what he could see. A big idol of the Mahadev was in front of him. He could observe some energy in Mahadev's eyes. Aryakt rubbed his eyes and looked at it again. The same energy was trying to say something to him and trying to talk. Aryakt moved his eyes, but the crowd around the temple made him tremble, and he again rested his eyes on Lord Shiva. Maybe due to the hunger or maybe due to his panic, Aryakt felt some communication happening. *Illusion?*

He looked into the eyes of Lord Shiva, which yet were closed. But now, he began to see them opening slowly. Very slowly. *Was it his hunger that made him see things like this?*

Aryakt then began to blink his eyes. The blink was slow. Very slow. Like there was enough time for the events to change drastically, Lord Shiva's eyelids opened slowly as Aryakt's eyelids closed slowly for a blink. This transition from open to closed had enough moments in Aryakt's life. He felt himself running twenty steps back to the old man selling vastra mala.

Aryakt saw him looking at him eagerly, wishing him to buy a packet. Aryakt just kept looking at the old man.

How old should he be? At least eighty years? Yes.

Someone called the old man, and he looked around. An old woman standing beside Aryakt slipped and started falling to the ground on her head. Since the time moved sluggardly, Aryakt had enough time to hold her from falling. Aryakt first hesitated to move forward, observing the crowd around. Then he thought for a while and started hesitantly to save her. The time then moved as usual, and she fell on her head.

The old man left his bag on the floor and ran to her. The old woman was his wife. People who were walking on the footpath gathered around her to help. Aryakt saw blood around her head. The muscle man leaning on the meat store's wall came forward in a hurry, pushed away the people around the woman, lifted her in his hands, and started running towards the main road for help.

As he ran, one of the glass pieces pierced his bare feet. He just stopped momentarily and continued running, holding the old woman. The crowd followed him.

Since they looked to be moving extremely slowly, even when running, Aryakt could move forward. He saw the muscle man feeling acute pain in his feet due to one of those glass pieces shattered from Aryakt's water bottle.

The autorickshaw driver was talking to his ten-year-old daughter at around a couple of metres away. She said, "The teacher asks me for the fees daily. Today is the last day to pay it, she said."

The driver felt pity for her and guilty himself. He emptied his pocket. The cash was around five hundred rupees, just enough for a month's fees. He then smiled to himself and said:

"Take this kid. It's enough for a month's fees. Remaining, I'll give in a week."

The girl innocently asked, "You have no more money left. Neither do Mom. Then how about the food at home?"

The dad bent down, hugged her, and said, "I have just filled the rickshaw tank with two litres of diesel. It is enough to earn some money. Don't worry. Okay!"

"Okay!" the girl said happily, walking towards the school.

The slow-moving time regained its pace, and the muscle man stopped at the driver and said hurriedly,

"She is the vendor of vastra mala at the Shiva temple. She fell on the floor, and he is her husband. Please help them get to the hospital soon."

The driver hesitated first for a moment and then regained himself back. He said:

"Of course. Get in."

The muscle man sat inside the autorickshaw holding the old woman in his strongly built hands. As the husband got into the rickshaw, the time moved slowly again. The driver asked the muscleman:

"Please inform their family."

The muscle man replied, "*They* are the whole family now. Their two sons have left them in an old age home. The couple sells these vastra malas to pay at least something to the orphanage. The sons are of no use. They don't pay anything" and continued,

"*We* have to get them to the hospital, and I can inform the old age home. Do you have some money to spend at the hospital for food for this person? I don't have any."

The driver looked at himself in the front mirror, thought for a moment, and said, "Yes, I do. He took out a fifty rupee note from the secret pocket of his trousers."

As Lord Shiva's eyes had just opened fully, Aryakt was desperate to look into those eyes. He tried opening his eyes immediately. But the time moved exceptionally slowly. He tried increasing his force to open the eyelids, but it was useless. Who can counteract time?

Aryakt, standing near the auto-rickshaw, heard the sound of the engine rhyming as it started. The smoke popped out of the silencer. He then gathered some energy and bent over to remove that piece of glass from the muscle man's feet. He forced him to get there soon, but the time moved slowly. Meanwhile, the old man bent forward and removed the glass piece. Aryakt felt disappointed. The old man thought to throw it away but held it back. Holding the glass piece tight in his fist, he sat looking at his wife with wet eyes.

Time moved at its normal pace, and the rickshaw started moving faster toward the hospital.

Aryakt, standing in front of the temple, opened his eyes fully and looked into Lord Shiva's eyes.

As the rickshaw disappeared, the crowd dispersed, murmuring. Aryakt turned around and found himself standing around thirty steps away, looking at Lord Shiva. Unknowingly, tears came out of his eyes. *Why tears? Was it because of the old man selling vastra mala at the age of eighty? Was it because the old woman fell on the floor by her head? Was it because their sons were indifferent to them? Was it because the muscle man was helping the woman unconditionally? Was it because of that glass piece of his water bottle hurting the muscle man? Was it because of that bright-looking girl worrying about her school fees? Was it because of that driver who emptied his secret pocket to pay the school fees? Was it his guts to take out the money he might have hidden to use for his emergency? Or was it the fact that the driver might not get any money for his ride to the hospital, which obviously would cost him some diesel out of the remaining two litres?*

Confused, Aryakt started crying and running to get into himself, who was standing facing Lord Shiva. The time moved slowly yet again, and the distance seemed impossible to attain in a lifetime. He tried moving himself faster, desperately, but he couldn't.

Aryakt moved his eyes below the face of Lord Shiva and was wondering while looking at the bluish throat. It was a light blue reflection that he saw. He knew the reason for it through reading, but he read that the blue colour was dark and intense. In contrast, it was light and pale as he started observing it. With this illusion of time and desperation, his observing ability had increased to multiple folds. Yet, he was as confused as he was surprised. *What next to understand?*

Aryakt, trying his best to run to get into himself, stood frozen when he saw a big group disturbing the traffic again. It was the group of people carrying the dead body for Antim Sanskar. Leading the group was a person chanting some mantras. Beside him was an eight-year-old boy with a fully shaved head holding his mother's hopes in his right hand.

The time again started to run at its normal pace. Aryakt had two options. One to get to himself quickly, for which he was desperate. The next was to get to that boy. His senses started pushing him to run towards himself, but as the one who stood observing the blue colour on Lord Shiva's throat realised that the colour started getting intense and thick, Aryakt chose the latter.

He ran towards the boy as the group was trying to divert the traffic for an easy movement of people carrying the dead body. Time again started moving slowly as he reached that boy. Aryakt bent his knee on the floor in front of that boy.

Everyone moved very slowly according to the time speed. But the boy was looking at Aryakt usually. It wasn't a slow motion. Aryakt then asked him:

"My kid, who is that lying there?"

"It's my mom."

Aryakt's heartbeat stopped for a moment. The blue colour started to look like an enriched and divine realisation. True and Intense. He placed his hand on that boy's shoulder and asked, "Do you have anything to say? Are you afraid now?"

The boy's reply made him despair. The boy said, "I have... No. I *had* a perfect hair. My mom said she'd set my hair like a hero for tomorrow's fancy competition at the school. But now I don't know. She might be sad or angry at me that I have shaven my head. I didn't want it to be shaved. Anyway, I'll convince her. She won't scold me. She is very nice. My grandfather says that she met God today and will be back tomorrow. I hope she is back by 8 AM. I have to get ready by then."

The intense and ecstatic blue colour started to misalign itself as Aryakt's eyes began to fill with slowly emerging tears in each eye. As his heart burst into a great cry, the blue colour settled itself again, even though two big teardrops were a transparent obstacle to the vision. *Why can't the time stop for a moment and run back for the kid to see his mother alive again, at least one last time?* As this thought came to his mind, the blue colour again started fading away.

The kid's innocent face has melted his heart. Is it the heart, or is it his reluctance towards people around? *What should he reply to that kid?* Even though the time moved slowly, he now had enough energy (maybe a more significant intent) to run faster and get himself into himself, who was standing looking at the Lord Shiva.

Aryakt, with closed eyes, unknowingly joined his palms as *Namaskara*. The gesture he used to do whenever he passed through a temple without completely understanding the meaning of it. Aryakt understood the definition of the bluish throat now. *Neelakantha* was in front of him. *Or was he inside him?*

Those two big tears started their journey down his cheeks. He wanted them to be there in his eyes forever. But he knew that the blue colour would fade with this very wish of his. So, he let the two tears drop and vanish. *Vanish into what? To disappear into that divine blue colour again.*

As he regained consciousness of being in this very world, the two tears scrolled down his eyes as if they scrolled down during his sleep whenever he dreamt about his mom and dad with him, being completely unaware of when those tears had started emerging.

Aryakt fumbled out of hunger, and the time moved as usual. He waited to see if it slowed back again. But it didn't. He looked around, and there wasn't anything like he had seen before. Every movement around was as if nothing had happened. He ran twenty steps back and saw the old man and woman selling the vastra mala. The muscle man lifts a big bag of chicken effortlessly. The autorickshaw driver was bargaining the fare of his next ride with a lady. The school bell rang, and kids moved faster to enter the main gate—no change in the circumstances.

The only change was in how Aryakt looked at Lord Shiva seated with closed eyes. He observed those eyes again and realised that they were always open.

❑

Chapter 19

Mohan's house was a two-storeyed building with a small and beautiful-looking lawn on the ground floor. Aryakt stood before the black gate and saw a board hanging on it. It read Advocate Gnanavel, with a long suffix of degrees. An XUV 700 was parked inside under a small chandelier.

Searching for the address of Mohan's residence was quite challenging for Aryakt, but the aura of the day's happenings on his mind made him break his barriers and talk to people. However, the question still was if it was the correct address that he ended up at. *Maybe Gnanavel is the son of Mohan*. That'll be the best possible thing, eliminating the need for another search. Aryakt exhaled deeply in hope.

As he looked at the building, he felt a gist of mystery around it, for some reason unknown. The afternoon with no one around the house, the sound of water droplets falling on the ground at equal intervals, and a weird silence surrounding the house made Aryakt feel keen. He just stood silent, facing the house for another ten minutes. Silence. Was it the silence before a storm? He still could hear the sound of water droplets. He just focused on it with his eyes closed.

"Nooooo...... I can see her. I can see her. She is here. Right here."

An old man came rushing to the corridor on the first floor and started shouting. Aryakt jumped across and hid behind the wall along the main gate. The old man looked around eighty years of age and quite tired. A man and a woman rushed into the corridor, listening to that old man, and tried to calm him down. They took him inside a room on the same floor and closed the door behind them.

Confused, Aryakt started to believe that the storm had started. *What if that old man was Mohan?* Aryakt spent another thirty minutes walking in front of the gate. He then saw a man coming out of the neighbouring house. Gaining some confidence, he stopped that man and asked,

"I am coming from Vishakhapatnam, Andhra Pradesh, and looking to meet Mr. Mohan. Got this address of him. Does Mr. Mohan stay here?"

The man looked at Aryakt from top to bottom for a moment. After getting half-convinced that Aryakt isn't a thief, he said:

"Do you see that board there?"

"Yes," Aryakt replied innocently.

"This person, Gnanavel, is an advocate. Handles criminal cases." The man raised his right eyebrow when he used the word 'criminal'. His haughty look made Aryakt shiver.

"Okay," Aryakt said, portraying a forcible smile.

Aryakt's expression was so plain that the man got himself fully convinced. Smiling, he said, "Mr. Mohan is his father. Are you their relative? I am unsure if any of their relatives stay in Andhra."

Aryakt's heartbeat increased. *So, the old man is indeed Mr. Mohan.*

The other man took his mobile and dialled Gnanavel's number. Once the call was answered, he informed Gnanavel about Aryakt's presence outside the house.

Gnanavel came out of the gate, and Aryakt's panic was again evident in the sweat on his forehead.

"Yes. Please," Gnanavel said questioningly.

The neighbour keenly was observing Aryakt. He probably was waiting to know who Aryakt was and his relationship with Mohan's family.

Aryakt couldn't find words to introduce himself. He trembled to talk. *How does he start? It'd be such an unusual way of introducing himself if he told the truth straightaway*. Instead, he said, "I..... My grandfather is.... was a friend of Mr. Mohan. I just came to meet him."

Gnanavel looked confused and surprised. He said, "Ooookay! But he is not in a situation to talk right now. Can you come later, please? Please give me your contact number. I'll telephone you whenever he gets better."

Aryakt's state of mind was evident on his face. His expression was filled with restlessness, confusion, desperation, and panic. He provided his contact number to Gnanavel and left the premises disappointed.

After a big fight with his fear, Aryakt could get into a nearby lodging in a single room. He didn't bother even to rest in a bus stand or a railway station. But he chose a lodge to bring himself closer to Mohan's residence. Having checked the cash he was left with, Aryakt felt a spike of insecurity. *Hotel Bill – unthought expense*.

At around 7.30 PM, Aryakt got a call from Gnanavel, and he stood up from his not-so-cosy bed at once and responded in extreme alertness.

Gnanavel said, "I am sorry to have sent you back in the morning. I didn't even ask your name. I am very....... Very sorry. My father isn't feeling well these days. I am upset, you know."

Silence for a moment.

"Hello. Are you there?" asked Gnanavel.

"Yes. I am here," Aryakt replied plainly.

"Well, can we meet now? Where are you staying? Any hotel?"

Aryakt felt a jerk in his mind. He replied vigilantly, "I am staying in Apsara Lodge."

"Well, I know that place. Do you mind if I come to your hotel room now?"

Aryakt felt a ray of hope in contrast to what he generally feels whenever he should talk to an unknown person. He replied with a little smile,

"That is fine. My room number is 154."

❑

Chapter 20

After disconnecting the call, Aryakt swiftly moved across the room to set things right as he was expecting a guest, which is a rare occasion. After around twenty minutes, Aryakt heard a knock on the door.

Gnanavel was dark, tall, and aged around forty-five. His smile, as he wished Aryakt, was the first thing that Aryakt noticed in him—*quite an attractive smile*. After exchanging wishes, Gnanavel came to the point.

"First of all, let me say sorry for being so indifferent to you during today's morning. It wasn't the best day today. I was so upset that I couldn't ask your name, at least."

Aryakt sat straight on the bed. Looking at Gnanavel, who was seated on the wooden chair, he said, indicating to himself, "Aryakt."

Gnanavel smiled in response.

"May I know what's the reason behind your visit? As far as I know, my father has no friends who live in Andhra. But I remember that long ago......" he stopped instantly and looked at Aryakt.

Hesitantly, Aryakt responded in the same way that he had rehearsed already. He said, "My grandfather, Mr. Srivatsa, passed away around three months back. Before he died, he had asked me to meet Mr. Mohan, your father, and talk to him."

"Meet my father? Okay. Firstly, I am sorry for your grandfather's demise. May I know what you would like to talk to my father about?" asked Gnanavel, looking at Aryakt curiously.

Aryakt was shocked, not with the question, but with the extreme curiosity with which Gnanavel asked it.

Since he had rehearsed the answer, he responded instantly, "My grandfather was in a coma for the last twenty-two years. He was back to consciousness three months back. He passed away the very next day. When I talked to him while he was conscious, he mentioned Mr. Mohan's name. I thought meeting him would be better as my grandfather wished."

Aryakt then looked hesitant about something that Gnanavel had observed clearly. After an uncomfortable silence, Gnanavel asked, "Is there anything else you want to tell?"

Aryakt, staring at his laps, looked at Gnanavel at once, had a calculated thought, and said, "Let me, please say something about myself, though there isn't much to tell. I was brought up in an orphanage since I had lost my parents when I was a baby, and my only relative – my grandfather was an army person. He had to be away from home almost throughout the year (Well, that's the best I could make out based on the circumstances since no one could validate my assumption). So, he had admitted me to an orphanage in Vishakhapatnam. When I cross-checked the records, I found Mr. Mohan signed as the witness."

Gnanavel's eyes got smaller, and he started thinking something. He thought awhile and asked, "When did it happen?"

"Probably around twenty-four, twenty-five years back," Aryakt said.

"Yes. In that case, I should be around twenty years old then," Gnanavel said and stood up. He continued, "Now, I get it. My father had been to Andhra for a couple of days. We never knew the reason for that trip. So, this should be it. And I remember another unusual thing during that time."

Aryakt saw something coming his way now. He asked in curiosity, "What's that?"

"Before my father went to Andhra, he had been on an excursion with two friends and was away from home for at least two weeks. We never knew where they went. Even now."

Aryakt controlled his increasing heartbeat and popping nerves. He spoke to himself, and to keep his out-bursting words in check, he murmured, "One fine day, what if the acceleration due to gravity of the Earth doubles its value? Would the world be the same? Do the oceans behave the same? Will the human tendency of movement and physical behaviour be the same? How about Satellites?"

"What?" asked Gnanavel, confusion on his face.

"Nothing. Nothing. I am just..... Warming up."

"Warming up for what?"

"Nothing as such. Please ignore. I get anxious at times. This tendency is from childhood, you know."

"Oh!" Gnanavel nodded understandingly.

"Will I get time to talk to your father?" asked Aryakt confidently.

Gnanavel thought for a moment. Having convinced himself, he said:

"Yes, but I think you should know my father's current state of mind."

The pitch variation in Gnanavel's voice made Aryakt understand that it wasn't a great thing. There was an untold pain (probably agony).

"Yes," he said.

Gnanavel exhaled deeply, took a cigarette from his pocket, lit it, and gestured to Aryakt if he minded it. Aryakt signalled a go-ahead. After taking a couple of intense puffs, Gnanavel explained:

"You might be wondering why I am sharing this with you. But believe me, there is no one with whom I can share this. I don't want anyone to make fun of my father. You seem to be a good man. And probably, my father and your grandfather are friends. So, it doesn't hurt me if you know about my father's situation. So, let me start here. My father is a writer. He writes novels. You probably know from your grandfather since he started writing when I was around twenty-one. Initially, he started as an article writer in certain magazines and shifted his interest to novel writing. It was fiction, but he did write some non-fictional books – biographies. He is successful as a writer, and his books do sell well. But he never looked satisfied with his writing. He was in search of something more. Something infinite (as he mentioned it to me). Something unexplainable. But in due course, we learned that there was a hidden aura of one person on his mind all the time, which he mentioned many times. It is a character from one of his novels. Initially, we thought it was usual for the writers to have their favourite characters among the ones they created. But it was something more than favouritism. It was like an addiction. It was like an obsession. That character's aura always made him take inspiration for his other books as well. Without that character's inspiration, he never had a lead character developed for his books. We knew that it wasn't normal anymore. We tried our best by letting him go through some psychology sessions with doctors, but they were of no use. It went on like that for years. Then, my mother passed away around a year back. It made him depressed. I thought he would come out of the aura, at least then. But it didn't happen. But now.... It is out of our hands. The doctor says it's not Parkinson's disease or any other neurological problem where people tend to have this kind of behaviour representing obsession with something or someone. It is out of our hands now."

After a moment's silence, Gnanavel continued, "I know how it is to be alone. It might not be the way you have grown up, but I felt left alone after my mother's demise. My father always was emotionally disconnccted from us after my mother left us. He is immersed in his world of books. My wife and son fill my world, but still, I feel the lag of not talking to my mother. You know, I can understand how you might be feeling. Feeling alone and left out. I am not sure if you do. You might be broad-minded, unlike me. Even though you are quite young, I feel it's hard to be alone. Or at least the feeling of loneliness."

Aryakt felt a gist of synchronising thoughts with Gnanavel. He, though, couldn't explain his state of mind. Then he asked something unusual, looking at Gnanavel.

"What's your father's pen name?"

Gnanavel looked at Aryakt in surprise, thought for a moment, and said:

"It's his original name. Mohan Ravindran."

"Oh. Alright." Aryakt replied.

Aryakt could feel the pain behind Gnanavel's words. The word 'Alone' had hit the absolute correct nerve and melted his heart. *I can help Gnanavel in some way*, he thought.

After that, the next question arose from his concern for Gnanavel. He asked, "Which character was your father supposed to be obsessed with?"

"It was from one of his initial novels. Incidentally, it is a biography that he had started writing, aiming to make it an inspirational story, and it ended up as a suspense thriller. The book's lead character had inspired him big time, and only then he had decided to write a book on that lead character."

"Biography?"

"Yes, it is. The book was about a girl who inspired the world around her in many ways. And she was the daughter of one of his very good friends named Prahlad. They stayed in Vatakara, and the story goes around in the same place."

"Interesting! What's the name of the character? Looking at Mr. Mohan's interest, he should have used the same name of the girl as his character's. Is it so?"

"Yes. You are right."

"And what's that character's name?" Aryakt asked curiously.

"Amita. Being specific on my father's thoughts, it's AMITA."

"Oh! Interesting. And what was the name of that book?"

"AMITA... What if she was here!"

❑

Chapter 21

Mohan should be a prime example of the most impacted author by his created character. Understanding *that* character isn't essential for Aryakt. But understanding Mohan's point of view is undoubtedly important. Continuing with Gnanavel's point, Aryakt asked:

"What had happened in recent days? Did your father's behaviour change?"

Gnanavel exhaled again as he took the last puff of his cigarette. He couldn't doubt Aryakt's genuineness as he could connect with the loneliness that Aryakt spent most of his life. He didn't feel any sense of fear in revealing his father's state of mind. After all, Aryakt and/or his grandfather were a part of his father's past. With utmost relief of venting out his thoughts, Gnanavel said:

"From the last month or so, his behaviour has completely changed. I think..... I think he is losing his mind. He is around eighty-three now. He says that he is seeing Amita in his room. He claims that she is visible for some time, and then she disappears," he continued,

"You may consider that he became delirious. But he had Amita's aura around him for the last thirty-two years. It's highly likely to imagine things, which is the core of this incoherence."

Aryakt stayed silent.

"Do you want to talk to him in this condition? It should be okay, I think since he is quite fine with his thinking ability."

Silence of a minute. Gnanavel understandingly waited for Aryakt to sort out his thoughts. Aryakt then said:

"How frequently does your father do this? I mean, claiming to be seeing Amita."

"Maybe once every two to three days. At times, alternate day. It is happening from a month from now."

"Well, okay. I'll meet Mr. Mohan after around a week from today. Will you be okay with it?"

"Of course, I am okay. I am okay even if you would like to talk to him tomorrow. The older memories may make him feel better. But what if he is unable to recollect your grandfather? Do you have his photograph?"

The word 'photograph' tickled Aryakt's mind, reminding him of his motto. He said, "No. I don't have any with me," and felt the humongous burden of lying to a genuinely caring person.

"Okay. So, you'd talk to my father after around a week?"

"Yes. I think so."

"I have a request for you. I still feel regret about the morning's incident. In turn, I would like you to stay at our home for the next week. We have a penthouse neatly maintained. You'll not have any discomfort." said Gnanavel.

Aryakt wasn't uncomfortable staying at an unknown residence but was hesitant. He then recollected the leftover cash and swallowed. He responded positively and said, "Thank you for that. But I would like not to be introduced to your father yet. At least I would like not to get into his eyes for a week."

"That shouldn't be a problem. My father mostly stays in his room, and we have another double room on the same floor where my wife and I stay. My father goes for a small walk every day and never gets onto the terrace. So, he never gets to the penthouse himself."

Aryakt smiled and asked surprisingly, "You are letting a completely unknown person stay at your home. Isn't it very generous?"

Gnanavel laughed aloud, "Well, your theory matches with my knowledge, and I can feel that you are a genuine person. Hence, I believe you," and continued,

"Come with me now. You can have dinner at the penthouse. Some servants can take care of you."

A penthouse again, murmured Aryakt to himself. This penthouse was bigger and had very sophisticated furniture. The view of the surroundings was quite dark during the night, obviously because of the dense greenery. Some lights were visible at distant places that looked like stars in the sky. The silence brought back the tranquillity that Aryakt's subconscious mind wished for.

A servant, neatly dressed, brought a delicious dinner for Aryakt. Aryakt felt quite overwhelmed with the kind of treatment he was getting. As he finished his dinner, Gnanavel got onto the terrace to wish him good night.

At around 10.30 PM, Aryakt retired for sleep as he knew the following day would bring him a plan to execute that might or might not work.

The piercing sunrays through the dense clouds were soothing for eyes as Aryakt walked along the railing of the big terrace and enjoyed the greenery around. Under the big almond tree, as it is easy to hide behind the leaves, Aryakt squeezed himself and observed the closed door from which Mr. Mohan got out into the corridor the previous day. At around 9 AM, a servant went inside the room with breakfast. In another fifteen minutes, the same servant started taking the stairs with the breakfast. Aryakt got into the penthouse immediately before the servant could enter the terrace.

"What's your name?" asked Aryakt as his curiosity had overcome his fear of talking to new people. He felt like reinventing himself with time. *Necessity is the mother of invention* – a theory that was proving itself.

"Sir, Prabhu sir," the servant replied smiling, his eyes avoiding Aryakt's eyes and staring at the breakfast.

Aryakt didn't wait anymore and asked his intended question.

"When does Mr. Mohan go for a walk? And does he go alone, or does anyone accompany him?"

"At times, I go with him if he asks me to. But there is no such order for me."

"When does he go for the walk?" Aryakt repeated his question.

"At around 5.30 AM," replied Prabhu.

"That is too early. Did you accompany Mr. Mohan today?" Aryakt asked, and Prabhu looked at him, questioning. Taking the hint of his doubt, Aryakt tried to cover up.

"Actually, my grandfather and Mr. Mohan are childhood friends. I came here to meet him. But, for now, do not let him know about my presence. I want to give him a surprise."

Prabhu looked at him indifferently and started leaving.

"Wait. How long does Mr. Mohan go for a walk?"

"Around half an hour"

Aryakt raised his eyebrows, and Prabhu left.

The following day, Aryakt got up at 5 AM, which was his usual time, and at 5.20 AM, he stood hiding behind the almond leaves and observed the closed door. At precisely 5.30 AM, it opened, and Mr. Mohan, wearing a white cotton kurta and a white cotton trouser, exited his room. With his delicate hands, he locked the door, then turned around and looked at the closed door of Gnanavel's family. With a stick in his right hand, Mr. Mohan started walking downstairs. The baby steps he took on the staircase showed his vigilant nature. *Not an ignorant person*. Aryakt, hiding himself from Mr. Mohan, observed Mohan go out of the gate and out of sight in a minute.

Setting right his hair and wearing the footwear, Aryakt walked out of the gate following Mr. Mohan. He observed Mr. Mohan talking to the vendor at a tea stall. Aryakt still hid himself from Mr. Mohan. In another five minutes, Mr. Mohan got up and started walking further. After walking around for half a mile, he turned around. Aryakt jumped across to hide himself out of Mr. Mohan's sight. He ran to the back of a general store and watched Mr. Mohan saunter towards his house. Aryakt followed him. Mr. Mohan had reached the house in another fifteen minutes.

Nothing peculiar, Aryakt thought. The day went as usual. Gnanavel met Aryakt at the penthouse before leaving for his office and after dinner.

"Do you want to talk to my father tomorrow? Do you need more time?" asked Gnanavel.

"It should be okay, I guess. How is Mr. Mohan doing?" asked Aryakt.

"Well, he is fine today. Can't say what's waiting tomorrow?"

"I understand. I have one request. I'll want to talk to him while you are at home. We don't know what'll trigger him."

"I think you are right. I'll be back home during lunch tomorrow. You can talk then."

"Alright. Good night," wished Aryakt.

As Aryakt retarded peacefully into sleep, he anticipated the next day might not be as usual as today.

The following day, Aryakt waited behind the almond leaves at 5.20 AM, and to his surprise, the door was locked already. He bent himself to check the door of Gnanavel's room. It was closed. The gate was closed. He ran downstairs and saw Mr. Mohan walking swiftly and taking a turn along a different path today.

Aryakt ran to keep up with his momentum and ensured Mr. Mohan could not see him. Gnanavel got up early and got to the terrace around 6.15 AM to see if Aryakt was up. He wanted to see if Aryakt wanted to talk to his father during the morning when he was very energetic.

He saw no one in the penthouse. He lit a cigarette and walked around the railing, waiting for Aryakt. After around five minutes, Aryakt came rushing onto the terrace and entered the penthouse without observing Gnanavel walking along the fence. Gnanavel saw Aryakt running into the penthouse. He waited for a couple of minutes and then knocked on the door. Aryakt opened it at once, and Gnanavel could see an extreme panic on Aryakt's face. His forehead was wet, and sweat rolled down like a waterfall.

"Are you okay, Aryakt?"

"I am ...... I am ...... I am not okay."

"What happened? Where were you all this time?" questioned Gnanavel, doubting his genuineness.

Aryakt closed his eyes tight, remembered the previous day's happenings, visualised the divine blue colour, murmured Faraday's law of equilibrium, and tried to control his trembling state of mind. He got up, took a glass of water, and poured it on his head.

Gnanavel watched him in surprise and as he thought to catch hold of Aryakt to know what he was up to. Aryakt gathered some air to speak out. He said, "I'll talk to your father, but not today. I'll have to wait at least a few more days."

Gnanavel's eyes narrowed, and he asked, "And why is that so?"

"I can't tell much more than this right now, Sir. But believe me. Please give me a couple of days more."

"Where were you till now? Tell me that first."

"Please don't ask me anything right now. I can explain it to you after a couple of days."

Gnanavel didn't believe Aryakt.

Aryakt drank a big glass of water and said, "Let me know if your father behaves differently today."

Gnanavel's eyes grew, and he asked, "What do you mean? Did you talk to him and or do anything to him?"

Aryakt felt a spike of fear. He said at once, "See. Listen. I have followed him during his walk. That's it. He didn't see me at all. I didn't talk to him at all."

"Then why all this drama?" asked Gnanavel.

"Believe me, please."

"Alright," said Gnanavel and returned to the first floor.

After around an hour, there was a shout from Mr. Mohan's room.

"Yes. I saw Amita again today. She is here. She is right here. Why don't you people understand? I have been seeing her for many days," Mr. Mohan shouted in ecstasy. It wasn't the fear. It was happiness in his voice. A rage filled with joy. Looking at his eyes was one of the most striking things for Aryakt. *Has he achieved anything? Did Mr. Mohan make out a way to talk to the dead? Or see the dead?*

Gnanavel and his wife came out of their room and held Mohan. Mohan was uncontrollable. He was shaking. His delicate body moved vigorously. He repeated the same set of words. Then suddenly, he looked upstairs and saw Aryakt in his eyes—*those deep eyes, the eyes that might have seen a ghost.*

Aryakt felt a gist of adrenaline mounting high.

"Can you see that person on the terrace?" asked Mr. Mohan, pulling his son and making him bend and look at Aryakt.

Gnanavel replied with a 'yes'.

"This unknown person is at our home, and you believe that. Then why don't you believe that Amita is in my room?"

Aryakt hid himself behind the railing and tried to settle his breath. The sight of those deep, tired, but presently ecstatic eyes of Mr. Mohan disturbed him altogether.

The sound of Mr. Mohan eventually decayed, and Gnanavel came to the penthouse.

"How did you know my father would behave like this today?"

"I didn't know that sir. But I asked you to please let me know if he behaves like that."

"That is what I am asking you. How did you guess it?"

Aryakt moved forward, held Gnanavel's palm with both hands, and said, "Sir, believe me. Give me a couple of days."

"Alright. But be careful. I cannot bear any mischief to my father."

❑

Chapter 22

Nothing was unusual the next day. But the next day, it was again the day of urge. The day of Mr. Mohan urging the people to believe him. The day when Aryakt was almost sure of the reason, Mr. Mohan shouted unusually. Aryakt might not know the cause to the fullest, but the occurrences around that reason were known. At around 10 AM, when Mr. Mohan's excitement settled, Gnanavel came to the penthouse. Aryakt was ready to talk to him.

Gnanavel and Aryakt sat on the chairs facing each other. Aryakt initiated the talk, gathering some guts. He said, "Sir, I have been reading books since childhood. Fiction, non-fiction, biographies, and so on. I might not know how a writer feels about his characters, but I can understand how they *could* feel." He continued,

"As you said, Amita being his favourite character, an obsession, to be rather specific, Mr. Mohan's *wish* is to see her. I don't know if he is seeing her, but I am sure he wants to see her."

"Do you agree with me here?"

Gnanavel thought for a while and said, "Maybe."

"Maybe. Okay! Now. When someone wants to see a person, he likes so much and who died thirty-two years ago, what's the way they have?"

Gnanavel stayed silent, thinking.

"Let me guess. They might want to see *that* person in someone else," Aryakt said.

Gnanavel nodded.

"And who is *that* someone else?"

Gnanavel remained silent.

"Think, Sir."

Gnanavel said, "Maybe someone else whom he loves as much as he loves that character."

"There you are. Yes. Someone whom he loves as much as he loves the character of Amita. Or it could be vice versa."

"Where are you trying to get to?" asked Gnanavel in a low pitch of voice.

Aryakt got up from his chair and started to walk around the room. As he walked, he said, "He needs someone to be with him, Sir. He needs the physical presence of someone around him. You are all there for him. But still, he is alone since no one is *with* him. As you said yesterday, being alone is hard. And the definition of being alone varies from person to person. We are all not the same. We think differently. We behave differently. We want different things. We love different things."

"What do you mean by 'he is alone'?" asked Gnanavel, getting up from his chair. He sounded worried.

Aryakt, in total contrast, was quite confident. He asked, "Do you go to his room anytime?"

"Not much," answered Gnanavel.

"Does your wife go in there any time?"

"Never."

"Do you have kids who get in there any time?" Aryakt shot question after question.

"My son is studying in Bangalore," Gnanavel answered in a plain low voice.

"See. Don't you think Mr. Mohan is alone? He lives in this big house. He has servants to take care of him. But does he have anyone to sit with him? Anyone who talks to him? Anyone who can spend some time with him sharing some thoughts?" Aryakt continued,

"Remember, Sir. He has been an author for the last thirty-five years. The line of sight of his thoughts could be much broader than yours and mine. And what does an author need? Someone who could understand their thoughts. Someone whom they could feel as a person with synchronous thoughts. Don't you think it is so?"

Gnanavel stood silent for some time and said, "My mother was like that. She used to be with him always. They shared many thoughts. As you used the right word, they had synchronous thoughts."

"That is right. You are absolutely right, and I have no other option but to believe it. Because every day, your father walks to the tea stall and then another half a mile ahead and back home. But do you know, on some days, he takes another route and gets to the graveyard where your mother was cremated?"

Gnanavel looked at Aryakt in shock.

"Yes. That is true. Mr. Mohan sits near his wife's grave and cries. Maybe he shares his popping thoughts with her. And obviously, he'd not get any response. And as you said, he frequently referenced Amita and never missed a chance to praise that character. Am I right?"

"Yes"

"So, for this very habit of his, which is accepted by the world now, he is using the character of Amita to get rid of his pain of not sharing his thoughts with anyone. He wishes Amita to be in his room, and if the world agrees, he probably wants to share his thoughts with his favourite character."

Gnanavel kept silent. After two thoughtful minutes, he said, "It is a complex situation. Do you think my father is assuming things? Some delusion?"

Aryakt exhaled and said, "I am unaware of his medical state. Doctors should confirm it. But I am sure he is looking for someone to share his thoughts. Having understood that you and your wife don't have enough time to spend with him, he is forced to look at other ways. But......." Aryakt stopped at once and kept silent.

"But what?" Gnanavel asked in curiosity.

"But I am not sure why he chooses only certain days to get to the graveyard. And why is he getting to the graveyard at all? For the kind of experience he has in writing, he should be able to visualise his wife being in his room. Maybe he wants to go out for a while. But that doesn't justify it altogether," Aryakt continued.

"Can you tell me any peculiar incident that happened after your mother's death?"

Gnanavel thought for a while and said, "Given the kind of analysis you are doing, I am not sure if I can recollect anything of such sort."

Aryakt almost fumbled on the bed as his knee hit one of its legs while walking, but he controlled himself from falling. He then said, "But we should believe one thing. The day he visits the graveyard is when he claims to see Amita in his room. Why can't Mr. Mohan be able to see Amita in the graveyard itself?" he continued.

"What if his claim is indeed true?"

"What do you mean?" Gnanavel asked in shock.

"I mean, what if Mr. Mohan *is* seeing Amita in his room?"

Silence.

Gnanavel said confidently, "I think we should get to the neuro doctor with this new information and see if the doctor can throw some light on it."

"I agree."

Gnanavel asked while leaving the penthouse, "Do you want to talk to my father after his checkup or before that? You seem to be knowing more about him now."

Aryakt recollected his original motto and looked for his bag. It was safely placed on the shelf. Well, it's better to talk to him after the checkup.

"Okay!" said Gnanavel and left.

Aryakt rushed to the bag and verified if the photograph was intact. As he opened the bag, his grandfather's smiling face was what he could see in the photo. The smile told him something. It took him to the day his grandfather told him about the secret. Specifically, it's not about the secret but the existence of a secret. *How could one have a secret hidden in a photograph? Will Mr. Mohan be able to recognise my grandfather? Does Mr. Mohan know about the secret? Will he be able to reveal it straight away to me?*

Mr. Mohan was just some footsteps away from Aryakt. Just a floor beneath. The answer to that secret could be so near as Aryakt could imagine. But then, what if he doesn't know about it? And even if he knows, will he be able to remember, recollect, and present it correctly with this existing mindset? He might also see Amita in the photograph.

As multiple thoughts popped up into Aryakt's mind, he felt restless. *Maybe people start lighting a cigarette in this situation*, he thought to himself and discarded the thought with a smile.

He thought about *that* one question that he asked Gnanavel about Mr. Mohan's peculiar behaviour after his wife's death. Aryakt thought it had something to do with Mr. Mohan's present behaviour. The death of his wife has something to do with his delusion, as Gnanavel presents it.

The entire day went in sorting out the thoughts around the same thing while keeping away the thought of the existence of any ghost in Mr. Mohan's room, or Gnanavel's room, or in the very penthouse he is staying now.

As he skipped his lunch, he was forced to have his dinner. Gnanavel was upstairs during the dinner and thanked Aryakt for the feedback that he gave. Gnanavel took it in a sportive way. He had agreed upon the primary issue that his father was likely to be going through, setting aside any other medical complications.

Aryakt couldn't concentrate much as his thoughts were masking him from taking any other information into his mind. He didn't know when Gnanavel left the penthouse, when he began to drowse in his chair, or when he fell asleep.

❑

Chapter 23

The following day, Aryakt woke up with a shout from Mr. Mohan.

"Why don't you understand that she is here? I am not lying."

Aryakt woke up at once from his chair, and as he got up with extreme backache, he struggled to stand for a minute. Somehow, he managed to get to the terrace railing and saw Gnanavel getting into his father's room, holding him. Then the sound decayed, and he closed the door.

Without further delay, Aryakt dressed, descended the stairs, and ran to the graveyard. He knew the exact place where Mr. Mohan was seated. He went to that grave and sat in the same place. He observed that the surface of the grave was clean. It should have been cleaned recently. So, Mr. Mohan should have come here again. *Most likely, today*. And hence he started shouting at home. So, it again validates his point that Mr. Mohan behaves this way only when he visits the graveyard.

What does happen when he visits this place? What will he get? Peace? Why does peace trigger his excitement? Does the ghost of Amita wander around here? But Gnanavel said that she died in Vatakara.

Is he forcing himself every day to come here?

The word 'forcing' had resounded in Aryakt's mind. A thought triggered a theory in him. He tried to validate it in his mind and got a perfect explanation. For its complexity and unbelievability, Aryakt had to discard it. He, however, didn't discount its probability.

He ran back home and got to the first-floor corridor for the very first time. He saw Gnanavel coming out of Mr. Mohan's room.

"Good morning. I observed Mr. Mohan behaving in the same way today," said Aryakt in a hurry.

With his head down, Gnanavel replied with a yes.

"Can you please come with me to the penthouse? I want to ask you something."

"Yes, sure."

"Please get your cigarette," said Aryakt, and then realised that it was not his business.

"But why?" asked Gnanavel in surprise.

Aryakt thought for a moment and said, "I heard that smokers think well while they smoke. I would like you to think well now. So..."

Gnanavel nodded and murmured, "I don't know what's happening here."

"Alright. Tell me, please," said Gnanavel, lighting his cigarette.

"Well, sir, do you remember your father mentioning what Amita looked like?"

Gnanavel thought for a moment and replied, "Not in specific. But if you read his book, then she was gorgeous. Extremely beautiful. Not sure if some girl like that exists."

Aryakt raised his eyebrows and tried to put his question better. He said, "I was trying to figure out if she looked like your mother. If you remember, I asked you whether Mr. Mohan started behaving any differently after your mother's death?"

"Oh! Was that your point? No. So, I haven't heard from my father or mother about Amita looking like my mother," Gnanavel said and stood silent while he inhaled a couple of puffs. He then continued,

"Well, for your question about any peculiar behaviour in my father after my mother's death, I noticed something there."

Aryakt looked at Gnanavel questioningly. "Yes?"

Gnanavel thought for a while and said, "After my mother's death, my father has dried his tears. At least that's what I thought. Whenever he remembered her, he used to cry. That is obvious. But I remember him sounding like he was crying, but tears wouldn't come out. I looked into his eyes often, but they weren't wet anytime."

"It happens, Sir. People do dry their tears. Given his age and experience, he might have dried his tears. The emotional quotient of an author, in general, is very high, but it isn't necessary for him to outburst those emotions in the form of tears. Maybe his tears were in his writing."

"Probably," said Gnanavel, leaving in a rush as his phone rang downstairs.

Aryakt kept thinking about what was probably making Mr. Mohan see Amita, if not because his wife resembled his favourite character.

Aryakt still believed that Mr. Mohan was forcing himself to do something. But for what reason? And what's that he is forcing? Was it getting to his wife's grave or seeing Amita? One of these two should be a 'forced' gesture.

Does an author's creation make him delusional? Could it be that Mr. Mohan was fascinated with Amita's character all the time. Why should he force himself to see her *now*? He could have done this for many years. From the time Amita died. But that isn't the case here. He started seeing her recently. Is it because of some neurological imbalance? *If that is the case, should I get to him with the photograph before his neurological problem worsens?*

Gnanavel is indeed a caring son. He isn't physically with his father all the time. Otherwise, he is a perfect son.

What was the title? What if..... What if she was here?

Aryakt got up from the chair in which he was seated. He ran down the stairs and requested Gnanavel to come to the terrace again.

"Sir, there is a way to know what's happening. I have an idea. Someone should be inside his room when he enters it after his walk. Preferably after the walk to the graveyard." Aryakt continued, "If you permit, then I can stay hiding, and I would like to see what he does in his room before Amita's name triggers into his mind."

Gnanavel nodded and asked, "How do we know whether he is getting to the graveyard? I can go behind him, but he may make out that I am following him."

"Exactly. Someone else should follow Mr. Mohan."

"Well. I'll let Prabhu do that."

Aryakt realised that it was the servant that Gnanavel mentioned. *He should be reliable*, he thought.

Gnanavel, Aryakt, and Prabhu were waiting on the terrace at around 5.15 AM the following day. The electric light in the chandelier was still on. The air still has the dew in it. The surroundings were still relatively dark. Mr. Mohan, with a stick in his right hand, opened the door, got out of the room, enveloped the surroundings, and locked his room. As he took the stairs down, Gnanavel indicated Prabhu. With his mobile on silent mode, Prabhu started following Mr. Mohan, quiet as a mouse.

As soon as Mr. Mohan turned towards the graveyard, Prabhu telephoned Gnanavel. Soon, Gnanavel unlocked Mr. Mohan's room and, along with Aryakt, got into it.

The room was free from dirt and disorder. The study table at one of the corners reminded Aryakt of his study table back at his penthouse, which he should vacate in another couple of months. That very thought made him feel sick yet again. He controlled himself and tried to focus on the current scenario. Aryakt turned around, and Gnanavel showed him a place to hide. It was near the big book rack covered with a velvet curtain. The rack and curtain were big enough for a person of Aryakt's physic to hide.

"Are you okay hiding here?"

"Yes. It is perfect."

"But please make sure that my father doesn't see you. His condition is not good these days, as you know." Gnanavel said in a helpless tone.

"Sir, does your father get to the book rack any time? Is there a chance for him to come to this side?"

Gnanavel exhaled and said, "No. Don't worry about that. He has the books for this month on the table. He never opens the book rack himself. Either Prabhu or I will help him take out the books that'll be sufficient for a month. It's been around a week since I took around five books. So, no worries. He'll not come towards the rack."

"Okay! I'll try not to make my presence felt. My mobile is in the penthouse," Aryakt replied confidently.

Gnanavel thoughtfully said, "If my father doesn't respond for half an hour or so, then I'll knock on the door and get my father into my room. You can then get out of here. I don't want you to stay here for long."

Aryakt thought for a moment and nodded. Both waited in the room for an uncomfortable fifteen minutes. Gnanavel's mobile then rang, and it was Prabhu. Gnanavel spoke for only ten seconds and disconnected.

"My father has been to the graveyard. He has started back home now. I'll get out of here. Please take care..... of my father." Gnanavel said and got out of the room and locked it.

It was scary for Aryakt to be alone in a locked room where there was presumably Amita's ghost. He turned around, still squeezing himself, and looked into the book rack. The transparent glass reflected the red velvet colour of the curtain. He looked into the glass, trying to notice if there was any reflection of a girl. *Generally, ghosts present themselves through the mirrors*, he thought to himself and discarded the thought immediately.

Then he started searching for what he called his favourite. For any book from aNoNyMoUs. Aryakt scanned through all the rows and columns but couldn't find any. Most of the books were classics and very old. Mr. Mohan had a vintage classic collection. *Why not? He is an author himself*, Aryakt murmured to himself.

The unlocking sound of the door made Aryakt turn back and stand in alertness. The following creaking sound of the door made him feel scared. Through one of the holes in the curtain that Gnanavel made, Aryakt saw through the shadow of an old man. And as the door was closed again, the shadow disappeared.

Mr. Mohan entered the room, kept his stick, leaned to the corner beside the door, and went near his study table. Setting the books in order, he walked around the room several times.

Whenever Mr. Mohan walked near the book rack, Aryakt could hear his heartbeat. He had latched his lips between the teeth to ensure he didn't make any noise. He sometimes stopped breathing when Mr. Mohan turned towards the book rack.

After several rounds of walking, Mr. Mohan turned on the light, and the room was bright. The tender sunrays piercing through the window were making the room still brighter.

Mr. Mohan sat on the bed silently for some time. Aryakt just observed Mr. Mohan from behind through the hole in the curtain. Mr. Mohan sat on the bed unmoved and started crying in a whispering sound, not aloud. The sound of the whispering cry was horrific for Aryakt. Was it Mr. Mohan or Amita crying?

Aryakt, being in confusion, tried to keep himself calm. He just observed Mr. Mohan keenly. In around a minute, Mr. Mohan struggled to get up. He stood up somehow and started moving his hands as if someone was in front of him, and he was trying to touch that person. He started murmuring, "Why do you come here only during mornings? And why do you want me to cry? Why do you not talk to me? My son... he is distraught for me. Why do you want me to shout your name when my son is home? I don't want to give him trouble."

Mr. Mohan stopped, wiped his tears, and then started murmuring again, "I shouldn't do this. I shouldn't do this. I'll not do this from now on. For my son's sake."

He then started crying in a whisper again. But this time, he was sleeping on his bed, covering himself with a blanket. It was evident that his physical ability was draining out as Aryakt saw him struggling to get the blanket on him. Mr. Mohan squeezed himself inside the thick blanket. Aryakt shivered, hearing the weeping sound from inside it.

❑

Chapter 24

After around ten minutes, Aryakt heard a knock on the door. Mr. Mohan slowly got himself out of the blanket and struggled a little to get out of bed. Staring at the emptiness, he moved his hands as if trying to touch someone. He then bent his head and opened the door. Gnanavel came in.

"How are you today, appa?" he asked, sitting beside his father.

"I saw her again today, Gnana. I saw her again today." Mr. Mohan said, holding his son's hand.

"Come on, let's go to the other room. We have a special breakfast today." Gnanavel said as he helped his father to get out of the room. As the left, Gnanavel turned back and indicated towards the curtain.

Mr. Mohan was looking happy to be surrendering his weight to his son. After a few minutes, both left the room, and Aryakt left and went to the penthouse.

Gnanavel, seated in front of Aryakt in the penthouse, felt dumbfounded. Shocked, he said, "So, is this house haunted by Amita's ghost?"

Aryakt kept silent.

Gnanavel kept silent.

Aryakt was thinking all the while about what Mr. Mohan had said to Amita. Looking at Gnanavel, he said, "I am surprised by one thing. Why did your father say, *why do you want me to cry?*"

Gnanavel started to explain again about how his father used to cry when his mother died and how his behaviour changed later. But Aryakt couldn't focus anymore. His blurry thoughts were slowly clearing up. A thought struck his mind like lightning. He went near Gnanavel, placed his hand on his shoulder, interrupted his talking, and asked, "Sir, does your father have friends?"

Gnanavel was surprised by this gesture from Aryakt. He looked at Aryakt's hand on his shoulder, but understandingly, he said, "Yes. He does have friends. Why?"

"Do they come to your home anytime?"

Gnanavel looked at Aryakt in surprise and said, "Not recently. But some friends used to come."

Aryakt nodded and asked, "Do they use to stay with him overnight at your home?"

"No. I never saw it."

"Another question, Sir. Did your family go anywhere recently, leaving your father alone at home? I mean for a day or two."

Gnanavel thought for a moment and said at once, "Yes. We did go to Bengaluru for a couple of days. To attend a function at my friend's home. My father was doing well then, and he insisted we go. Prabhu was taking care of him for those two days."

"Well, well. Did Prabhu stay with your father for the entire day?"

"No. Only for part of the time, but he used to attend to my father promptly or at least telephone him. But he used to come in person to serve him the food."

"Food. And that's prepared by?"

"A cook stays in the room at the back of the building. She never comes to our home. Prabhu serves the food to my father."

Aryakt tried to connect the dots. He asked, "Does she come to your father's room anytime?"

Gnanavel tried to determine the chances of that happening and said, "Unlikely. Quite unlikely."

"One last question, Sir. Did you observe that Mr. Mohan's behaviour changed from when you were back from Bengaluru?"

"Yes, it is that. Exactly that. But why do you ask these questions? Are you doubting Prabhu or the cook?"

"No. If you want to check the CCTV camera recording, I am sure you'll find someone entering Mr. Mohan's room during those two days. Maybe someone unknown to you. And known to Mr. Mohan."

Gnanavel stood up and asked, "What'll that mean?"

"I'll tell you. But I am shocked. Mesmerised rather. Presently, is your father in his room?"

"No. He is with us."

"Sir, please give me the keys to your father's room and let me sit inside it for at least fifteen minutes."

"But why?" Gnanavel asked in restlessness.

After around twenty-five minutes, as Gnanavel curiously waited for the door to open, Aryakt opened it and saw Gnanavel standing on the terrace, his face hidden behind the almond leaves. Aryakt recollected his image of standing in that position and waiting for the door to open.

Gnanavel raised his eyebrows and looked at Aryakt questioningly. Aryakt just smiled and started taking the stairs to the terrace slowly. Even though his face looked tired, his smile said his mind wasn't. As he tried to speak, his voice fumbled to create any sound. He got inside the penthouse, had a glass of water, washed his face, and returned to Gnanavel.

"Sir, we should check the CCTV camera recording."

"Yes. Prabhu is getting the memory stick now. But what's the matter at all? What did you figure out in these twenty-five minutes? Did you see........" Prabhu interrupted Gnanavel as he brought the memory stick.

"Let us check this," Gnanavel said with authority.

Prabhu connected the memory stick to the laptop and sorted the videos by date. Gnanavel selected the specific date when they were out of town.

During the evening of the first day, at around 7.30 PM, Mr. Mohan and another person entered the house and then Mr. Mohan's room. Mr. Mohan was quite friendly with him. But Gnanavel couldn't recognise him. His face wasn't visible since he always was looking down.

As the video continued to play, Mr. Mohan got out of the room multiple times, probably for some fresh air, but the other person never came out.

The following day, at 5.40 AM, Mr. Mohan got out of the house, obviously for a walk, as per his usual schedule, and the other person remained inside. Mr. Mohan returned at 6.08 AM. At 8.40 AM, Mr. Mohan and the other person exited the room. Mr. Mohan shook hands with him, and the other person left the house. No one else came into the home during those two days.

Gnanavel looked at Aryakt with widened eyes and said, "How did you know this?"

"I didn't know it, but I could only guess someone came into your father's room during those two days."

"But how did you guess it?"

"Sir, whatever happened had happened during *those thirteen hours* when the other person was inside your father's room."

Gnanavel asked Prabhu to get downstairs and held Aryakt by his shoulders. Pleasingly, he asked Aryakt, "Please tell me Aryakt. What's wrong with my dad? Is it any black magic or something? Don't hesitate to tell the truth if you know it already. Do you know what that person did during those thirteen hours?"

"Yes, Sir. I know it."

Gnanavel, with his mouth opened in surprise, looked at Aryakt.

"Then tell me," he demanded.

"Sir, he had painted a picture of Amita on the wall right in front of your father's bed."

Gnanavel's eyes narrowed as he keenly looked at Aryakt. He then said:

"What?! Where is it? I didn't see any picture."

"It has always been there, Sir. Always before your father's eyes as he sat on the bed."

"Let's go and check." Gnanavel started moving, and Aryakt stopped him.

"You'll not be able to see it now. For that, you'll have to......" Gnanavel interrupted Aryakt and said:

"What do you mean by *not being able to see*? If you try to take advantage of my amiable nature, don't forget I am a criminal advocate. I am going to......."

Aryakt held him by the shoulders and made him sit on the chair. In a delicate pitch of voice, he tried to explain. He said,

"Sir, the painting is done so that one can see it through their tears. Not without the tears in the eyes."

Gnanavel's eyes narrowed as he tried to absorb the words. He said in confusion, "But how? But how is it possible? And why all this......? And who is that person?"

Aryakt held him and said, "I know the answer for 'why.' But not for 'how' and 'who'."

"Then tell me why?" asked Gnanavel, who was losing his mind.

❑

Chapter 25

The tea stall vendor was surprised, looking at Gnanavel, seated on the chair, waiting for a cup of tea. A successful advocate always holds a high-class stature among the masses. However, Aryakt and Gnanavel took their cups of tea and started walking into the greenery. Aryakt then explained.

"Sir, I believe that the person with your father during those two days is a well-wisher. Definitely a well-wisher. And he should have understood your father quite well. I think this is what would have happened." Aryakt said, took the last sip of his teacup, and then continued.

"I am unsure if he was Mr. Mohan's friend for a long time. But a friend. He is also an extraordinary painter, as you can figure out the finesse of his art. Mr. Mohan might have shared his thoughts with him. As you know, he had to. The other person always heard him with patience and understood that Amita's aura in your father's life is unexplainable. There was not a day that he spent without remembering her. At the same time, his thoughts are not the ones to be contained. They wanted to explode. Explode into the words. But he needs someone to catch his words. He needs some validation for his thoughts at times. But having lost his wife, he also had lost that validating mind of his thoughts. And this person – this new (probably) friend of his had all the time in the world to listen to your father's thoughts."

"The new friend had understood that Mr. Mohan had stopped having any tears in his eyes after his wife's death. He also understood that Mr. Mohan had reduced crying because of his maturity in understanding life. The only pain for Mr. Mohan was to lose *that* validating person of his thoughts. Days are changing, audiences are changing, kids have grown up, and the means of communication are changing. How an author of his calibre, who is still around the aura of Amita (which he might be fed up with at times), who lost his wife – a soulmate and the only person who shared his thoughts, could retain his physical or psychological ability?" Aryakt stopped for a moment and continued,

"The new friend understood Mr. Mohan's state of mind. He should have been in a situation where he must leave Mr. Mohan's acquaintance soon. But before he left, he wanted to present a good gift to his dear friend. He executed it and made it so great that Mr. Mohan started believing it as reality."

"So, he painted her on the wall? But why exactly?" asked Gnanavel in a shallow pitch of voice. Aryakt felt surprised to see him talk so plainly, childlike.

"As I understand it, Sir, *that* friend thought Mr. Mohan would feel happy seeing Amita. But already Amita is a virtual reality for Mr. Mohan. The new friend didn't want to intensify that aura of hers. So, he chose a way such that Mr. Mohan, if at all, cried for some reason, and tears filled his eyes, which obviously meant that he was unhappy with something. So, if he is unhappy, what's that one thing that can make him happy again?"

Gnanavel, without any further thought, said, "Amita."

"There you are. So, the new friend painted Amita's picture in such a way that one can see her image only when one has tears in his eyes. How could he accomplish such a thing? But that is surely a masterclass. But........"

"But what?" Gnanavel asked as his heartbeat increased.

Aryakt could feel the panic on Gnanavel's face now. The sweat on his forehead proved it. It was not a usual feeling for Aryakt. He could understand the situation of Gnanavel. Aryakt stopped instantly, turned towards Gnanavel, and said:

"No need to worry, Sir. Let me complete."

"But the intention of the new friend didn't work as he thought. Mr. Mohan observed that he could see Amita whenever he was crying. Crying with tears in his eyes, which wasn't happening these days. So, Mr. Mohan had figured out a way. If the presence of Amita made him happy, then the absence of his wife made him sad. Extremely sad. That sadness made him cry *with tears*. As he understood that crying was making him see Amita, he started visiting the grave of his wife, and that made him emotionally very sad. He would cry thinking of his wife, and tears automatically filled his eyes, and he would be able to see Amita on the wall. As the eyes get wet, the painting seems to move around randomly, but her smiling face is visible if you can focus well. That's what I did, sitting in Mr. Mohan's room for twenty minutes. To cry and observe Amita's painting." Aryakt continued,

"Mr. Mohan then made it a habit to cry so that he could see Amita. And this habit is not what his new friend would have anticipated."

"But how does the new friend know what Amita looks like?"

Aryakt smiled and said, "One is an author, and the other a painter. Both are extraordinary in their respective professions. If an author can imagine things and convert them into the art of writing, then a painter can grasp that imagination and create the art of painting. Don't you think so, Sir?"

Gnanavel stayed silent as he could not figure out the words to explain his state of mind. He could only say one thing, which Aryakt didn't expect at all.

"I would like to see Amita once."

Aryakt understandingly nodded his head and said, "But for that............."

Gnanavel interrupted, "I know what is to be done."

Both arrived at Gnanavel's home in about a quarter of an hour.

Another quarter of an hour passed.

Gnanavel got down the stairs from the terrace exceptionally slowly. There was no hurry. He knew Amita wasn't going anywhere. He entered the room, looked at Aryakt leaning on the terrace railing, and closed the door.

Gnanavel didn't need to struggle much for what was necessary for the moment. Just reiterating Aryakt's explanation and imagining his father's situation made his eyes wet. Tears started flowing down his cheeks. As he lifted his head and looked towards the wall, he saw a gorgeous face smiling at him. A smile that made him smile in turn. As he realised what the new friend did for his father, he lived in an ecstatic moment where the smile and tears would burst simultaneously.

Wiping out the tears, Gnanavel came out of the room. Looking at Aryakt, he smiled similarly to how Aryakt had smiled some time back while coming out of the room. Getting onto the terrace, Gnanavel hugged Aryakt in ecstasy and thanked him for making him realise that his father hadn't gone mad. He is pretty healthy.

"I should....... I should not only be thankful to you Aryakt, but..... but I should feel lucky that you came here. But why? But why are you here? Who sent you here? I don't know how to thank you, Aryakt!"

Aryakt didn't say anything. Gnanavel thought for a moment and said, "Let us go now, and you can talk to my father. Let me do something for you."

Aryakt, immersed in Mr. Mohan's situation, was momentarily indifferent to his own situation. When Gnanavel reminded him of the matter, he at once realised that the challenge had just begun for him. Unmasking the actual motto, Aryakt said with little effort, "Yes, I do. Yes, I do. But…. "

"But what?"

"I'll want to talk to him in private, please," Aryakt said, observing Gnanavel's expression keenly.

Gnanavel said smiling, "That is alright. Let's go"

Aryakt held Gnanavel's hand and said, "Sir, not now. Let your family know about the mystery of Amita. Let your father know that he is very fine. Tell him that *waqt ke deemak ne iss author ke dimag ko khokla nahi kiya*"

Gnanavel laughed in happiness as Aryakt felt extremely happy seeing Gnanavel come out of all the confusion he had regarding his father. Gnanavel left the penthouse in ecstasy.

The relief in Aryakt's emotional conscience triggered the most important thing he had been missing all these days. As his hands shivered, he could hardly hold his mobile. He struggled to synchronise his fingers and move them accordingly to dial Mugdha's home telephone.

"Sir, how are you doing? Any problem, Sir? Where are you?" asked Mugdha with an excitement of talking to her teacher after a long time and equally concerned about his whereabouts.

Aryakt in response said, "I am doing good Mugdha. How are you and the other kids?"

"We are……. We are good, Sir," said Mugdha plainly.

The following sentence that Aryakt said clarified to Mugdha that he was doing fine. She then was happy for her beloved teacher and an excellent guru. Aryakt said,

"You might have completed the composite mathematics by now. Go through the introduction of Trigonometry once again. We can deal with its applications in real-time scenarios once I am back—one request. Check with the other kids. Vilohith was quite interested in his science project. I.... I am unable to be with him right now. He shouldn't lose the focus, please. He needs continuous motivation."

❑

Chapter 26

Gnanavel left his father's room, indicating Aryakt with a smile. In the silent room, Aryakt could hear his heartbeat. Mr. Mohan sat in silence with his head down. Aryakt was trying to find words to start his point. Gathering all the energy, he said:

"Sir, I........"

Mr. Mohan said at the same time, "Aryakt. Interesting name."

Aryakt looked at Mr. Mohan, and he stared at his deep eyes. They were tired. They were intelligent. They were innocent. They held dreams in them.

"Yes, sir," Aryakt smiled.

Mr. Mohan adjusted himself in the chair again and started with a little laugh, "I am confused now about who should get the first appreciation. Probably not you."

Silence.

"It should be my friend, Harshvardhan." Mr. Mohan cleared his throat and continued, "The painter. My mistake. The great painter. I believe you acknowledge this. Will you?"

"Yes, sir," Aryakt said, twisting his fingers.

"You have proven to my family and relatives that I am not mad. And to me, you have proven that Amita isn't around here. She is either on this wall, hidden, or in my mind, again hidden. Hahaha. Well. But the impact of the non-existence of someone taking over the impact of their existence shouldn't be humanly acknowledged."

Aryakt nodded in agreement.

Mr. Mohan raised his eyebrows and said, "So, you understand my talking. People generally fear to talk to me when I am emotionally active."

"I get it, sir," Aryakt said in a low-pitched voice.

"You deserve a standing ovation, Aryakt. But I am unable to stand right now. I had my lunch just now, you know."

Aryakt got up from his chair and went to Mr. Mohan. He said, "Sir when I first heard about your Amita, I could only feel the generosity of an author to live one of his characters. Isn't it a fine line that divides one's addiction and one's love towards a person? I think you had that clearly defined line until you saw this painting. Isn't it, Sir?"

Mr. Mohan looked at Aryakt, startled. They exchanged a smile that held many meaningful words in it. Breaking the next minute of silence, Mohan said:

"But firstly, let me know what you wanted to talk to me?"

Aryakt started to panic as Mr. Mohan held his hands with his thin hand, which had lost its elasticity and volume.

Aryakt has been waiting for this moment for a long time now. Considering what he had gone through, the few days were very long for him. He picked up his bag from the chair and opened it. As he touched the photograph, his mind started toggling and jumping around various thoughts.

The validation for his grandfather's words would be here, now. *What if Mr. Mohan doesn't recollect Aryakt's grandfather? He should be Mr. Mohan's friend. One of those friends in the picture is definitely Mr. Mohan. But does his mental condition mask his older remembrances?*

As his heart started beating faster, he took out the photograph and looked at it himself. The smiling face of his grandfather made his heart melt. His grandfather's dear friend was with him now. Thoughts popped around about how happy his grandfather would have felt had he been here right now! He didn't want to hold any more time for making Mr. Mohan happy.

Aryakt then gave the photograph to Mr. Mohan. His eyesight was quite good, and he didn't have spectacles even at eighty-five. Mr. Mohan looked at the photograph keenly, rubbed his eyes, and looked at it intently. He then saw Aryakt in surprise.

The colour on his face had faded, and his hands started shivering. His lips started turning white. Mr. Mohan signalled Aryakt to come near him. Aryakt went and sat in front of him with bent knees.

"Who....... Who...... Who gave you this?"

Mr. Mohan's pitch of voice was draining away. Aryakt felt like calling Gnanavel at once, but Mr. Mohan held Aryakt's hand tight.

"My grandfather, Mr. Srivatsa," Aryakt said, pointing to his grandfather's face in the photograph.

"Are you..... Are you...... You are here. Did you come here with this photograph? To me?"

"Yes, Sir. Shall I call Mr. Gnanavel?" Aryakt asked in a hurry.

"No... No... Do you know one thing? I never expected that you'd come. God is great. How is Srivatsa doing? I.... I really cannot believe this." Mohan said as tears rolled down his cheeks, and he touched Aryakt's face affectionately.

Aryakt could feel Mr. Mohan's anxiety. He stood up and went out of the room to call Gnanavel. Gnanavel came at once, and both went to Mr. Mohan.

"I am fine. I know what brought you here. You are.... You are here....." Mr. Mohan could not catch his breath, and words fell short for him in the present situation.

Aryakt felt extremely surprised and afraid by seeing Mr. Mohan's changeover in behaviour. Something big had certainly triggered him. Aryakt looked at the photograph as his keenness multiplied.

Gnanavel started to lift Mr. Mohan to take him to the other room. He said, "I think we should get him some sleep. I'll call a doctor home."

As Aryakt and Gnanavel helped Mr. Mohan to walk to the other room, Mr. Mohan started talking aloud, "I can tell you what you want. I can tell you that. I know what you want."

Aryakt's heart came to his mouth. He was almost there. Mohan could reveal the secret anytime now. Aryakt slowed down a little, but Gnanavel was in a panic. He was ignoring anything that Mr. Mohan said.

As they reached the other room, Gnanavel made Mr. Mohan sleep and gave him some medicine. Seated beside his father, Gnanavel asked him to calm down. Mr. Mohan was looking at Aryakt with a smiling face. He brought himself to steadiness after some time. Gnanavel insisted on getting to the hospital, but Mr. Mohan discarded the idea.

As Gnanavel was convinced that his father was doing alright, he got up. Mr. Mohan, with a smiling face and big eyes (those eyes weren't tired anymore; they were bright. Very bright), asked Aryakt to come near him. Aryakt sat on the bed beside him, and Mr. Mohan said, "Gnanavel is worried about me. I ought not to get into secret talks now. I'll talk to you tomorrow morning. Well done, my boy!"

Confused, Aryakt left the room. Excitement and panic were fighting their way inside Aryakt's mind, and neither of them subsided for another hour. Again, the word 'secret' brought itself to the forefront.

It was 7 PM, and Aryakt just wished for the clock to keep ticking faster and faster as it was sure that Mr. Mohan hadn't lost his mind and was quite sensible. Whatever lies inside the photograph was very much known to Mr. Mohan. After all, he was one of the friends in the picture. But his response to it made Aryakt overwhelmed. It was as if Mr. Mohan knew Aryakt forever.

A greedy feeling, which was not like himself, evoked inside Aryakt and pushed him to get to Gnanavel's room, knock on the door, and talk to Mr. Mohan right away. *Just tell me, what's that secret?*

Prabhu, who came in with the dinner, spoke to Aryakt for the first time in a friendly manner. He was always reserved and portrayed that servant's gesture of not looking into the owner's eyes. *I was never the owner*, Aryakt thought.

"Is Mr. Gnanavel home?" asked Aryakt.

"Yes, Sir. He is with his father." Prabhu answered.

"How is Mr. Mohan doing now?" Aryakt asked curiously.

"He had breathlessness during the evening, and we got a doctor home. He had suggested to get some tests done tomorrow."

Aryakt then realised that he had slept for some unknown time when he didn't know anything else was happening on the first floor. He nodded.

After dinner, he waited for Gnanavel and dozed off into sleep at some unknown time.

The secret is just a night away from me was the only thing on his mind.

Early in the morning, it was quite a rare incident when Aryakt woke up with some disturbance around. He saw the time, and it was 4.25 AM. Some noise on the first floor increased as time progressed. It was Gnanavel who was talking loudly. Aryakt cleaned his face and rushed to the terrace railing. Gnanavel was crying aloud.

Aryakt's heartbeat paced like a cheetah as he ran downstairs. There was no need for him to get permission to enter Gnanavel's room. What he saw was not what he wished for, even in his nightmares.

Mr. Mohan was dead.

Aryakt was shaken up. Unknowingly, both his palms touched his head. Technically thinking, an eighty-five-year-old person passing away isn't such shocking news. But he was alright the previous day. Did the photograph do this to him? Did Aryakt's very presence do this to him? He couldn't stop himself from asking these questions, and every thought led him to believe that it was because of the photograph, and his mention of Mr. Srivatsa made Mr. Mohan overwhelmed by something.

Gnanavel got up from his bed and saw Aryakt standing in shock. He got to him at once, hugged him, and cried aloud. "Appa is no more Aryakt."

At times, guilt has this enormous energy over any other feeling around. It can dominate the best and worst feelings of life. Aryakt hadn't tasted it anytime, but this moment had *that* bitterest feeling of guilt in him. A lovely son like Gnanavel, who deserved to be with his father after Amita's episode, was again brought to a tragic situation. Aryakt knew he *was* the reason for it. His guilty feeling was shooting up.

What made him feel ashamed of himself was Gnanavel's response to it. It seemed like Gnanavel never thought of it like Aryakt. He didn't blame Aryakt even in his thoughts.

Aryakt stood at the door's entrance and saw Gnanavel, his wife, and Prabhu crying. Such a lovely family and a great son! – and on the other hand, he was the person who was responsible for bringing this tragedy to them. Given his physical condition, Mr. Mohan should have lived at least for a year more. The first thought that Aryakt had when he entered the room was regarding the secret that's still unrevealed, and probably, he'll never know it. Did he think about what Gnanavel's family had lost? No. Guilt. Guilt. And Guilt.

He started feeling the blue colour getting misaligned. It began to fade away. He still felt like he was standing on the road. Gnanavel's cry, which resembled the cry of a kid, brought Aryakt back to the situation.

The feeling of guilt was so bitter that Aryakt ran onto the terrace and vomited. His eyes turned red as he looked into the mirror. His forehead was still clear with no sweat on it, which surprised him. He realised that guilt suppresses any other feeling - even the panic - the panic that had come as a trait for Aryakt by birth.

❑

Chapter 27

The following day, Aryakt packed his bag and cleaned the penthouse, arranging the things in their proper places. It was the time to leave. Aryakt did enough at Perambra. He let alone the topic of the secret and started making up his mind.

Gnanavel, who was entering the terrace, saw Aryakt ready to leave. He asked plainly, "Are you leaving for Vizag?"

"Yes, sir. I can't stay here anymore. I blame myself for coming here, and I feel I am responsible in some way for this tragedy."

Gnanavel felt surprised by Aryakt's words and understood his guilt. He said in response, "Don't say that. You are not guilty. Rather, you made us feel my father didn't lose his mind. Truth should be unveiled. You made my father feel the same. Imagine if this incident had occurred before we knew about the painting. We would have been under the impression that my father had some neurological issues. Such a shameful lie that could have masked that beautiful truth. By the way......" He thought for a moment and continued,

"Dad was mentioning something about a photograph yesterday to me. I am unaware of what it is exactly. But he was very excited about it. He says there is some secret in it."

Aryakt remained silent.

"Look, Aryakt. I can't force you to stay back. And I don't know what else is going on in your life. But one thing. If you have come this long to know the secret behind that photograph, then I can understand the importance of it to you. My father was pleased, in fact, after knowing that you were the grandchild of his childhood friend. His mere excitement had shown that the importance of that photograph was unquestionable. And I know what you might be thinking now. The only person who had the answer to that secret is no more now. And believe me, he hadn't said anything to me yesterday. But my friend....... You should believe one person now."

Aryakt lifted his head at once and looked into Gnanavel's eyes.

Gnanavel said, "Yes. One person. And that is yourself. In this house, you have done something we might never have done. Can't you do the same for your own life? Do not give up on this important thing in your life. I am ready to help you. Think for some time. You can make better decisions."

Gnanavel waited as Aryakt had put his bag on the chair. He then said, "Thanks for your kind words. You are thinking very big of me. But I am not so generous, Sir. I am afraid of that secret now. What holds in it is a mystery, but how about its impact?"

He exhaled and continued, "However, it is inevitable now. I am destined to look for it. Solving and knowing the secret is one part of it. But trying seems to be inevitable. Sir, there isn't much for me here now as your father is no more. But one piece of information may help."

Gnanavel set right his dhoti and asked, "Yes?"

"Do you know any other childhood friend of your father?"

Gnanavel thought for a moment and said, "Yes. Mr. Somasekhar. He lives in Perambra, and he is my father's childhood friend. You can meet him. I'll let Prabhu take you there. Wait."

Aryakt thanked Gnanavel. Prabhu and Aryakt started to Mr. Somasekhar's house, around eight kilometres from Gnanavel's.

Mr. Somasekhar was around the same age as Mr. Mohan but looked around ten years younger. He was bald on his front side, and the untidy white hair at the back of his head was hardly visible. One of his front teeth popped outwards whenever he opened his mouth to say something. Somasekhar's habit while talking was to make fun of things around. He laughed at every other sentence of his.

Aryakt thought that the popping tooth represented his humour quotient.

"Gnanavel told me that you are coming here," he said, seated in a room that looked too old for the kind of house they were in. The house was marvellously built with top-notch modernity. The architecture was eminent, and the outlook was a pleasure to watch.

"Yes, sir. I am Aryakt."

Somasekhar laughed a little and said, "Interesting name. You might wonder why this room is so old-fashioned when the house is so modern. Aren't you?"

"No, sir. Yes, sir."

"Hahaha. I like it. Not the room. But your *No, sir. Yes, sir,*" Somasekhar said and continued, "I like my room to be like this. I live in the present moment, but do not forget my past."

Aryakt nodded.

"Now tell me. What can I do for you?"

"Sir, I am Mr. Srivatsa's grandson. And here is a photograph that he gave to me. Do you know anything about it?" Aryakt said as his heart started coming to his mouth, anticipating an exuberant behaviour in Somasekhar looking at the photograph. Aryakt wasn't in a situation of taking another shock for the moment. Hesitantly, he handed over the photograph to Mr. Somasekhar.

To Aryakt's surprise, Mr. Somasekhar laughed aloud.

"It is a bliss to see my friends. We have had very few photographs back then, you know. Mohan, Srivatsa and Satyavratha. Three excellent friends. I don't discount myself from the group, but *they* were indeed very good friends."

"Do you know anything about this photograph?" Aryakt asked curiously after being convinced that Mr. Somasekhar wouldn't faint after looking at the photograph.

"Well, Well, Well. I know what you are thinking. You seem to be quite intelligent. I know your mind goes to the question about who clicked this photo. Isn't it? And you anticipate it was me? Aren't you?"

Aryakt never had that thought in mind. But he just smiled in response.

"Hahaha. See. I can catch all your thoughts. But no. It wasn't me. It should be some random person walking on the beach. I know. I know. If they go on an excursion, they'll not take anyone with them. I am sure of that."

Aryakt asked at once, "Why is that?"

Mr. Somasekhar suddenly looked at Aryakt with intensified eyes—a rageful look. Aryakt jumped on the chair at once. Then, a sudden changeover. Mr. Somasekhar laughed aloud at once. He said, "You would like to know all the secrets. Hmmm....."

Aryakt just smiled and nodded his head. Mr. Somasekhar was again normal (coming out of the animated laugh zone). He said, "The three friends never spoke to others much. I was the only one whom they used to speak to. They were reserved most of the time. And for an excursion, there was no way for them to be with any other person. The journey and company mattered to them, not the destination. They wouldn't allow some random thoughts of someone to disturb their patterned thoughts."

"Sir, do you know anything about this photograph?" Aryakt asked in a plain voice.

"Hahaha. Its.... It's a colour photo, my friend. Hahaha," the room resounded with Mr. Somasekhar's laugh. He then again became normal and said:

"I know what you are asking. I did not see this photograph at any time. But I remember these three friends went on an excursion at some point. I don't remember when, but they definitely went on an excursion. There was some mystery associated with that."

Aryakt looked at him desperately.

He continued, "Hahah. See. How eager you are to know. Hahaha"

This guy is a .... Aryakt stopped himself from completing the sentence. Instead, he smiled flatly.

Back to being normal, he said, "I remember asking them about where they are going. But they never disclosed it, which was weird. But yes, for your question, I don't know about this photograph. But......." He looked at Aryakt keenly.

Aryakt made sure that he didn't show up desperate. He contained himself to be normal. Mr. Somasekhar then said, "See. You are becoming ignorant now. This is modern-day youth. Eager a moment back and ignorant a moment after. But I live in *that* very moment. Not before and not after."

Aryakt now understood why the old man was left away from the house but not in it.

"Well, yes, sir," Aryakt answered as he started to lose his patience, and it seemed like there was nothing he would get from Mr. Somasekhar. Then Mr. Somasekhar said something unexpected.

"But these three friends aren't normal people. Depending on one's perception, they were special in their own way. I must say, they were special and extremely good human beings. I know them very well. I don't easily appreciate people, but these guys deserve it."

Aryakt looked at him in confusion.

Mr. Somasekhar's voice became a little heavy, and he said, "See, kid. I don't know why you would like to know about this photograph, but I can tell you about the three friends and their peculiar mentalities. By the way, Mohan died yesterday. We haven't been meeting now for years. It was sad to know, and we are growing quite old. So, these things happen. How is Srivatsa doing, by the way? Should be very old."

"My grandfather passed away a couple of months back, sir. And before that, he was in a coma for the last twenty-two years. He met with an accident back then," Aryakt said with his head down.

Mr. Somasekhar remained silent momentarily and said, "That is a true tragedy. I am sorry for that. My friends are all nearing now. Do you know where Satyavratha is?"

Aryakt moved his head.

"Okay. I don't even know where he is now. Where did Srivatsa, your grandfather, die?"

"Vizag. Vishakhapatnam."

"Okay, Andhra. Maybe after he retired from the Army, he settled in Andhra. Surprising," he said and continued:

"See Aryakt. I don't know what your grandfather said about this photograph and why it is important for you to know about it. I won't ask because I know I'll be unable to throw any light on it. But......"

Aryakt looked at Somasekhar in desperation and immediately corrected his expression. But the little time lag was enough for Mr. Somasekhar. He said:

"See, again. You are toggling between eagerness and ignorance. Why do youth nowadays toggle so much in their behaviour?"

Your say about toggling behaviour is ironic since you toggle more than anyone else, Aryakt thought to himself and smiled.

"But let me tell you one thing. There is something peculiar with the three persons," said Mr. Somasekhar and continued, "They have their way of expressing things. Something very unusual. Something that made others always feel peculiar about them. Not the same trait, but similar impact."

Aryakt looked at him with a plain face. He had no expression, even though his mind was racing like a cheetah to know what that peculiarity was.

"Let me put it straight for you. You'll have to be careful with Mohan. He'll include your character in his next book if he finds you interesting. He observes people a lot. Their behaviour, their reactions to things. He judges people based on what they laugh at. It's not exactly judgemental. But he always wanted to show the readers the reality of this world. Even his fiction has relatable characters; the one from whom he got inspired to write a character would know that while reading his book. Very observant. And equally expressive in writing."

Aryakt, with his narrowed eyes, concentrated on Mr. Somasekhar's words.

"Coming to Satyavratha. He is a man of principles. The peculiarity in his behaviour is something unique. He never lied to anyone. Not even to some unknown person. If he says something, then it must be true. Or the other way around. If only a thing is true, he says it. He sometimes confused us by asking us to figure out something when he was silent. He never lied to anybody, even for minute things. His extreme truthfulness made him seem devoid of emotions, but he wasn't that kind. He was very intelligent and fair to everybody. At the same time, he was very reserved. He spoke to minimal people. Something was indeed great about Satyavratha."

Aryakt was flowing with Mr. Somasekhar's words and tried to imagine what Mr. Satyavratha looked like.

"Now coming to Srivatsa. I know you are waiting for it. But it would help if you held your breath tight before knowing his peculiar quality. I keep the best for the last."

It was quite a long time since Aryakt didn't feel sweat on his forehead. But this warning-like statement from Mr. Somasekhar made him feel panic again. He looked around and tried to readjust himself in the chair.

"Srivatsa was a tricky person. Instead, I should put it this way. He loved tricking people. I don't know if you are aware of this since you say that he was in a coma for a long time. But you should know it, Aryakt. Your grandfather was an interesting person. People used to be excited and pissed off with him at the same time. You know, he used to trick people bizarrely."

Aryakt held himself tight, expressionless. The thought, *What if he did trick me as well?* was exploding inside him, but he ensured he wouldn't give away this time.

"Srivatsa used to lie. Lie selectively. There is a peculiar way of expressing things. He would utter the exact converse of information and let the other person figure out the information.

When he had to mix the truth and lie at once, the distinction may be in words or expressions, and he may change his body language to convey the lie. It started as his technique to fool people but got to a stage where he did it effortlessly. And then he did it inevitably. He used his words to tactfully build a story with truth and lies like a spider builds its web. He did this with everyone except his other friends, whom you see in this photograph. I am sure he was quite selective with this behaviour with his colleagues in the Army. There should be a certain level of cunningness, and that's again perception."

Mr. Somasekhar exhaled profoundly and said, "So, a big caution, Mr. Aryakt, about your grandfather's words. I don't know if that habit would persist after being in a coma for twenty-odd years, but it is likely for a man like Srivatsa. An uncompromising character."

He gave Aryakt some time to absorb what he said. After a few silent minutes, when Aryakt could only try to escape the shock, Mr. Somasekhar said, "Lastly, I haven't asked you about what your grandfather said. And this is the reason for it. It doesn't matter what the summary of his words is. What matters is what he said *exactly*. I hope you did understand."

Aryakt got up from his chair without a word and started moving out of the room. Mr. Somasekhar approached him, held his hand, and said, "Don't worry, kid. Remember that your grandfather is not a liar. He tricks people. But he *is* trustworthy."

Aryakt thanked Somasekhar for spending time with him and clarifying some critical things that only *he* could have done. Mr. Somasekhar walked with Aryakt to the main gate, and when the silent Aryakt said goodbye to him, he said, "See, again, your behaviour toggled to silence. You know, silence is also a behaviour if one can feel it. Don't toggle again before you start leaving."

Why didn't you mention the fourth friend, whose expression is equally peculiar? Why did you discount yourself from that legacy, sir? Aryakt thought. Instead, he said, "Thanks a lot, sir," and left the premises.

❑

Chapter 28

Madhava was getting ready for his evening meeting of the day. In a couple of days, he had an important meeting with one of his new clients that had the potential of an opportunity to hire around fifty employees. As a CEO of a small firm, this client was critically important.

On the other hand, Sameer was to visit his counterpart team in Switzerland in another three weeks. Visiting Switzerland had always been his dream. Sameer's excitement was quite evident in his behaviour at the office. His colleagues cracked jokes with him, and some were silently jealous.

The marriage proposals had already started for Sameer. It was just started for Madhava. They, however, were softly pushing it further. No such personal commitment they had with anyone that held the potential to turn into a marriage proposal. So, an arranged marriage was the only option.

At around 6 PM, Madhava got a call from Aryakt when he was driving home in his newly bought Duster.

"This isn't pleasant anymore since you had already restricted us from calling you but delayed calling us yourself. How are you, Babumoshai?"

Aryakt whispered, "I am doing okay, Madhava. One thing......."

Madhava couldn't hear Aryakt's words well. He said, "Wait. I am going to connect the phone to the car's Bluetooth. I'll also connect it to Sameer."

Aryakt waited in silence.

Sameer's teleconference with his counterpart was just done, and he was to start soon from the office and do some thermal wear shopping. As he got ready to move from the office, he saw the mobile ringing. It was Madhava.

"Hey, buddy. What's up? Want to join me for some shopping?" he said in excitement.

"I know. I know–Switzerland trip. No one can hold you in one place these days. By the way, our Power star is on the call."

Sameer felt a gist of happiness bigger than his excitement for shopping. He said, "Hey, Aryakt. How are you, and where are you?"

"Hello, Sameer. I am good. How are you?"

"Good man. You didn't answer the other question."

"Well, I am in Kerala," Aryakt replied dryly.

Madhava took his Duster to the left and stopped it at once. Sameer replaced his lunch box on his table, and both were immediately on alert. Sameer waited for Madhava to respond.

"Kerala?" Madhava asked.

"Ye... Yes," Aryakt said.

Silence.

Madhava thought for a while, and Sameer realised it.

"Are you in some problem, Aryakt?" asked Madhava, getting himself close to the car steering as if it were the microphone.

"Yes," Aryakt replied hesitantly.

A spike had raised in the heartbeat of both friends, almost in synchronisation. Sameer opened his Google Pay app and was ready to send money if needed.

"Tell us what happened. Aryakt" asked Madhava.

Aryakt wasn't sure why he dialled Madhava's number, but probably it was the only number he could dial. He spoke what he truly felt. He didn't hesitate this time. He needed someone around him who could understand his situation.

"Will you both be able to come here?" asked Aryakt hesitantly.

Without hesitation, Madhava said, "First, tell us what you are up to right now. Are you at a safe place?"

"I am safe. Don't worry. But can you both come to Kerala?"

"But what happened, Aryakt?" asked Sameer.

"I can't tell it on the phone. But please try to come." Aryakt said and continued, "And can you............"

The friends waited for Aryakt to complete. But nothing came from his side. Then Sameer asked, "And what?"

"I don't know how to ask. But can you please lend me some money? I cannot go to the place where I am staying now. I'll have to get to the hotel."

"Shit," Madhava murmured.

Within half a minute, Aryakt got two messages, with thirty thousand being credited each time.

Aryakt couldn't control the popping tears. He felt thanking his friends would not be any respect for them. It should be something more significant. Instead, he asked, "How did you ensure each sent me the same amount? Were you prepared for this?"

"Not at all," said Sameer and continued.

"Which place is it in Kerala?"

"It is Perambra. The nearest railway station is Calicut." Aryakt said as some confidence was building in him, listening to his friends.

"And the nearest airport as well," said Madhava, and Sameer replied, "Yes. That is true."

"We'll be there tomorrow by lunchtime. Sameer, I'll call you later today," said Madhava and disconnected the call.

The friends knew that Aryakt wouldn't bother them for minor reasons. There should be something big and something vital.

Sameer and Madhava met at the Vizag airport at 10 AM.

"It is surprising that Aryakt went till Kerela. Anyway, I'll do my summer shopping there." Sameer said.

"You see. Records have started to break. I have postponed my meeting with the new client next week."

"Let him face some problems, you say?" Sameer asked as they got the boarding pass from a beautiful woman at the airport counter.

"Don't you have any check-in luggage? We could have waited a little longer at the check-in counter," Madhava winked.

"Well, no, sadly," Sameer replied, smiling.

"And yes, Aryakt should go through some challenges. He has been having problems all the time, you know. Converting them to challenges is what is important."

Sameer raised his eyebrows, and both got through the security check.

After around one hour, as they both got into the flight, Sameer asked, "What do you think is waiting for us in Kerala?"

Madhava didn't reply and started to think. Finally, after some time, he exhaled deeply and said, "Don't know. But whatever it is, it should be more interesting than our office stuff."

"Why not?!" Sameer said as the flight took off, manifesting the aerial view of the beautiful city of Vizag.

Right before the lodge, Aryakt stood excitedly, waiting for his friends. As he checked the time, it ticked precisely 2 PM. A taxi stopped beside him, and his face glowed with happiness. Aryakt always had the problem of not clearly showing his state of mind—especially his joy. The feeling always was held masked behind his anxious mindset. But, this time, it wasn't like that. As Madhava and Sameer exited the taxi, Aryakt ran towards them and hugged them at once.

"Oh. Oh. Is it you, Aryakt?" Madhava asked, smiling.

"Apsara Lodge. What a classic name for a lodge!" Sameer said, and the three friends burst out into laughter.

Apsara Lodge has a reasonably big terrace and is accessible to customers. After lunch, at 4.30 PM, the three friends walked on the terrace. Aryakt tried to explain the previous week's happenings to his friends, covering the essential instances.

The two friends heard him without speaking a word. As the instances proceeded, they just felt awestruck. Finally, when Aryakt had mentioned the peculiar behaviour of his grandfather, Madhava laughed aloud and said:

"Not to discount any of the things you have gone through, I feel that I missed meeting such a person who tricks others with the mix of his truths and lies, still maintaining the reputation of a 'good man.' That's just wow!"

Sameer was still absorbing the content. He asked, "Is that painting on the wall still there?"

Madhava was expecting this from Sameer. Aryakt replied, "Should be, yes."

"Wow! Unbelievable. What an experience it would be!" Sameer said in astonishment.

Madhava looked at Sameer and raised his right eyebrow. Sameer nodded as he felt Madhava saying, "*See, records started breaking.*"

Both patted Aryakt's shoulder, but he couldn't accept the appreciation. The only thing on his mind was the peculiar behaviour of his grandfather. He said in a worried tone, "Now, I don't know if all this I am doing is true. I mean, is it necessary?"

"What do you mean?" asked Madhava as the hotel servant brought three teas to the terrace.

"My grandfather could be lying about the secret in the photograph," Aryakt said.

"Oh yes! What could be that secret?" asked Madhava.

Sameer answered instead. He said, "That person was in a coma for twenty-two years. Do you think he'll even remember who he spoke to and how he used to speak?"

Aryakt nodded and said, "I know what you are pointing out at Sameer. But remember, his friend, Mr. Somasekhar, said it is likely."

"Biologically, it might not be likely Aryakt," replied Madhava.

"But, what if?" Aryakt asked.

The friends thought for a while, and Aryakt said at once, "If Mr. Somasekhar's words are to be believed, then we have to do one thing."

Madhava and Sameer looked at Aryakt keenly. *Where is he getting to?*

"The way that my grandfather used to trick the people was by lying to them. And when he had to convey something that had both lie and truth hidden, he used to trick them in *how* he spoke. So, the whole trick was either in using the words or in the style in which the information was conveyed. Maybe he used peculiar words to convey a truth and some other kind to convey a lie." Aryakt said.

"Trick with words," said Sameer.

Aryakt, looking at the floor all the while, nodded in disagreement and said, "Not only the words but trick with expression. Words being one of the means of expression."

The friends got confused.

Aryakt said, "When I think of the time I was in hospital, being there was not so natural. I have been emotional, that is agreed. But my grandfather wasn't emotional. Yes, he wasn't, for me at least. He was ecstatic – not for seeing me. Being ecstatic after coming out of a coma. Can you arrange the sequence?"

"What sequence?" asked Madhava.

"Happiness is when we win over something. Ecstasy could be one of those conditions where we lose to something but still feel the happiness of winning. This isn't so easily realised emotion. *He was patting his chest when I saw him through the door.*"

"As per you, what did he lose, and what did he win?" asked Sameer.

"I can't say exactly. But I can only guess. My grandfather might have realised that he had lost most of the years of his life. Maybe he had something important to do." Aryakt replied.

"And what he won?" Madhava asked.

"He could have recollected *that* important thing that he should do. It's a winning card for him." Aryakt said and continued, "And then, in the ecstasy, he played his expertise. He played the game that he was an expert at. Don't we all do that when we are ecstatic? Do something that you are an expert at."

"And what did he do?" Madhava asked, throwing his empty teacup into the dustbin.

"The one classic thing which he was expert at. Tricking people. And who was there in front of him to talk?"

"You," said Sameer, confused.

"Exactly. Talking to me about something was very important for him. And he had used his age-old tried and tested trick on me." Aryakt felt happy and sad at the same time. Happy because he could deduce something out of the confusion. And sad, thinking about what more deductions he must make, unaware of what's waiting next.

"It's looking like you are playing a game. It's not how life works. What you have been doing from last week or so isn't normal, Aryakt." Sameer said.

"But what other option does he have?" asked Madhava.

"He should continue what he was doing. No. No. Carry on." Sameer corrected himself instantly.

Aryakt just walked around the terrace thinking about something. Madhava asked, "What do you want to do now? How can we know what the truth was and what was the lie in what Mr. Srivatsa, the great, told to you?"

Aryakt looked smiling at Madhava for his question. He replied, "Reconstruct my grandfather's dialogues, phrase by phrase. Word by word. Expression by expression, and then deduce the truth and lie."

❑

Chapter 29

Post midnight, at 1 AM, the two friends were ready to hear what Aryakt had to say. He had thought a lot and tried to reconstruct Mr. Srivatsa's exact phrases, words, and expression during those ten minutes.

"What a memory you have got, man!" Madhava said, looking at a book filled with Aryakt's analysis.

"Still, I think I am missing something here," Aryakt said, looking at his writing.

Sameer and Madhava took the book and read the page with the heading 'Summary.'

The weird sound of his laugh, his shrank pupil expanding, the highly unusual aura inside the ICU. It's top of my mind as I try to recollect it. Here is what he said.

"I have something to tell you."

"Bring my bag."

"This is very important."

"Listen to me carefully. There is a secret in this photograph."

"There is a treasure you'll get if you can crack that secret."

Then he shouted something as I was leaving the ICU.

"Don't neglect it. It's very important for you."

Madhava and Sameer read it twice and with extreme curiosity. Sameer said, "Are you sure Aryakt that these were his exact phrases?"

Aryakt looked tired. He raised his eyebrows and replied, "I think so. I have spent around four hours recollecting it. And this is what I think the phrases were. They should be ninety percent correct."

"The context isn't changing anywhere. It is all about the secret in the photograph," said Madhava.

Sameer added, "If any statement is considered false, then others might still hold good that there is a secret in this photograph."

Madhava thought along Sameer's lines and said, "What if the statements related to the 'secret' and 'treasure' are the lies?"

Aryakt's heart came into his mouth. Sameer looked at Madhava in shock.

"No. No. I am just guessing. But think, it could be as well, true."

Aryakt nodded as he thought about something. Sameer said, "If those two statements are lies, why is this photograph important to Aryakt? 'Important' is used in two sentences."

"How about those two being lies? Say, the photograph is not important at all," Madhava asked.

"I thought you would say that. So, if the secret is true, does he think that the secret doesn't hold any importance? Also, the treasure should not be of any importance or value." Sameer said thoughtfully.

"If something doesn't possess a value, then is it called a treasure?" Madhava countered.

As the two friends made some permutations to deduce something out of those sentences, Aryakt interrupted them. He said:

"Now I know exactly. That's it. We.... We are concentrating only on the words and phrases. It is my mistake, though, that I didn't recollect it. It was always there right in front of me. Now I know the meaning behind his wild laugh. I know what it is that I missed recollecting."

"What?" asked both the friends in synchronisation.

"The expression. An important factor of my grandfather's traits. Not only the words but the way he said it. Now I know. Let me rephrase them."

Aryakt took the notebook from Madhava and started writing something in it. The two friends stood beside him as he used the terrace railing to support his writing.

It took him around twenty minutes to rephrase the sentences, and the friends waited patiently. Aryakt said at once, "See here, friends. As he spoke to me, trying to convey some important message, he couldn't, I think, get over his age-old and successful trick. After seeing me in the hospital, he might have thought for a while and developed a way to use his trick. We do not know how his expression changed when he was healthy. Maybe with his body language, some signs, or something else. But being on a bed in the ICU, what change in the expression that he could give? I know what he did," he continued as the friends listened to him curiously.

"He stammered."

"Stammered?" asked Sameer.

"Yes. Stammered. I remember my grandfather stammered a lot, but not always."

"It could be a natural tendency of a patient awake from coma," said Madhava.

"Could be, yes. Then why did he laugh so wildly after completing the sentences? It was an exuberant expression like after one achieves something big," Aryakt counter-questioned.

Aryakt continued, "As I recollect, all his phrases were stammering. I remember filling his stammer with various words. When he stammered at 'sec,' I helped him complete that word by using various words starting with 'sec,' and then he stopped me at 'secret.' And this happened at every sentence."

Sameer held his head and said, "This is confusing, Aryakt. So, if stammering is the way of his expression, then are all the phrases you wrote lies?"

"They shouldn't be because the photograph is true. It is right here. So, whatever he said, stammering should all be true," Aryakt answered thoughtfully in a low pitch of voice.

"In that case, what is the lie here?" asked Madhava.

Aryakt was silent for a moment and said, "That is what I am trying to figure out."

Sameer was losing his patience and said, "I think the theory of your grandfather tricking people itself is a lie. And even if it was true, he might not have used it while talking to you. After all, he was conscious after twenty-two years. The stammering, as Madhava indicated, could be a natural thing."

Aryakt wasn't convinced yet. He believed that his grandfather was tricking him. His laugh – it wasn't a normal one. It had disturbed him for many following days. *Yes, it wasn't a normal one. He thought there was a trick and some big lie was hiding somewhere.*

As Sameer and Madhava were on the edge of getting convinced that no lie lies in those phrases, Sameer said, "See Aryakt. Don't get too lost in Mr. Somasekhar's words. *He* might be lying. Who knows?"

"Let us sleep now, Aryakt. It's very late. We'll stay here tomorrow as well. Don't worry. Let us figure out something tomorrow," said Madhava, and the friends started walking downstairs.

As they walked down two floors, Aryakt held Madhava by his shoulders. He shouted, "I remember now. Oh my God!"

"What's the matter, Aryakt? Why are you shouting? People are sleeping around. It's 1.20 AM." said Madhava, trying to close Aryakt's mouth with his palm.

Aryakt asked his friends to get onto the terrace again. They ran back upstairs. As they reached onto the terrace, Aryakt said aloud.

"Friends. I don't know how to say this. I am.... I think I'll go mad. I am terrified now."

"Control mister. What's the matter?" said Sameer worryingly.

"There was..... Yes, he spoke only one sentence of his without stammering. Yes, only one. Without any stammer at all. Clear like a crystal and with confidence. And that should be his only lie during the conversation. He played a trick, certainly. The stammering was an act of expressing the truth. The photograph in my hand is the proof of it."

Madhava and Sameer looked at him with narrowed eyes. Madhava asked, "What's that phrase?"

Aryakt was controlling his stammer. The phrase that was going to change the whole circumstance of his life. Air bloated from his mouth, but the words didn't come out. He forced them out.

"The very first sentence that he spoke to me. I forgot to recollect it; that was the only sentence without a stammer. He said, *I am your grandfather. Do you remember me*?"

Dead silence on the terrace for a moment.

Aryakt felt his forehead sweating. It was the first time he felt panic while being with his close friends.

Sameer came out of his sleepy mood and said, "So, it means........"

Aryakt nodded and said in a low-pitched voice, "Yes, Sameer. It means that he is not my grandfather. Mr. Srivatsa just tricked me. He isn't my grandfather at all."

❑

Chapter 30

Sameer, standing near the cash counter of a nearby restaurant, waited for Madhava. The cashier looked at him and asked, "Sir, if I may ask you something. You seem to be tense."

Sameer looked at him and smiled. The cashier was neatly dressed in an ironed cotton shirt and trousers, with a red tilak on his forehead. On the contrary, Sameer looked pitiful without proper sleep during the night, unbathed yet.

As Madhava came to Sameer with three Masala dosas packed neatly, Sameer asked him to move.

"I think the sleeping pill is working well. I haven't seen anyone take it. It was just in the movies that they showed that it works. It's 10 AM now, and Aryakt is still asleep." Sameer said as they walked towards the Apsara Lodge.

"It is good for him to sleep for a while. He is hugely disturbed." Said Madhava as he realised that he had forgotten to take the chutney.

"Don't bother. It is Masala dosa. So, it's okay. Chutney can be optional," said Sameer and continued, "But Maddy, tell me one thing. How likely it is for an eighty-plus-year-old person to trick someone right after getting to consciousness after being in a coma for twenty-odd years."

Madhava stood silent for a moment and said, "Not sure."

Sameer clicked open the door to see if Aryakt was awake, but he was in a deep sleep. Madhava checked Aryakt's bag and took out the photograph. Sameer sat beside him.

"Secret in a photograph! Isn't it fascinating? Isn't it one of those classic fantasy stories where a great magician realises his son based on a photograph he possesses?" asked Madhava, looking keenly at the photograph.

"Hmmm. Fascinating. But what's the secret here? Is it the place where it was clicked? I mean the beach. It's beautiful, though." said Sameer thoughtfully.

"It seems the beach is almost empty. Only the three friends. None on a beautiful beach during sunset. Does it make sense?" asked Madhava.

"What do you mean?" Sameer asked at once.

"Is it possible for a beautiful beach to be almost empty during the sunset? Where are the tourists?" asked Madhava, looking surprisingly at Sameer.

Sameer nodded and said:

"It was taken around twenty-five years back, at least. Mind you."

"Well, yes. The tourists at that time might not be as many as we see today. But an empty beach? Is it a proper assumption?" Madhava asked, nodding in disagreement.

"So, what are you trying to say? Do you think it's a morphed photograph?" asked Sameer, looking at Aryakt, who started to move a little on the bed.

"Sameer. Think once. With what Aryakt told us about his lying grandfather, the scope of ridiculing anything should not be discounted. Don't you think so? I mean, what if the photograph itself is a lie? What if it is....." Madhava was lost in some thought.

Sameer waited for Madhava to finish his sentence. But he didn't. Sameer then asked:

"What if it is.... what?"

Madhava said, "What if it is a painting but not a photograph?"

Sameer felt astonished and took the photograph from Madhava's hand. He observed it minutely and said, "It's not a painting, Maddy. One cannot paint it with such a detailed finesse. It should be a photo capture for sure."

"It's not a painting. It *is* a photograph indeed. Not because there aren't great painters out there, but because my grandfather stammered while saying it is a photograph."

Sameer and Madhava looked at Aryakt at once, and he was awake. Sameer smiled and said, "So, you think one can paint with this finesse."

"Of course. Do you remember the painter who painted Amita on the wall? And you know how one can see it. If that can happen, then why not this?" Aryakt said as he got down the bed.

The name of Amita had triggered a wave of mystery in their minds. Madhava got up from the chair and walked around the room in confusion. Sameer just watched him think and didn't disturb him. Another fifteen minutes passed as Madhava and Sameer waited for Aryakt to be in his routine.

"We didn't see that wall. Isn't it?" said Madhava, raising his eyebrows at Aryakt.

Aryakt was thoughtful at Madhava's point but focused on another topic. He didn't answer Madhava but stayed silent, wearing his cream cotton shirt as if getting ready to go somewhere.

"Well, I know that you have said goodbye to Mr. Gnanavel. But if we aren't facing any more surprises (maybe he meant that the idea of finding the secret is discarded for any reason whatsoever) and are into our routines, then before we leave

Kerala, we should go to Mr. Gnanavel's home and have a look at *that* wall."

"Very true. Very true," agreed Sameer.

"You might have wished for something at the wrong time, Aryakt. There is a saying, *Be careful with what you wish for; you might get it*," said Sameer as he played with a tennis ball standing amid a dense forest.

Aryakt was seated on the ground, plucking the grass, and Madhava looked around and took pictures. The forest was on the outskirts of the town, where there was immense greenery, and the density of trees made it look like a forest.

"Why do you say that?" asked Madhava without turning his face from a tall tree and trying to focus on a peculiar-looking bird.

Sameer said, "Simple friends. Doesn't it look so flat now? Just a photograph in hand, correction, in a bag. With no one to validate if it has any secret. And even though it has a secret, what treasure will he get? And given the circumstances surrounding various lies, will the treasure be definite? Is it for good? Or is it for bad?"

Aryakt looked at Sameer in shock. Madhava still tried to focus on the bird, almost getting near to the tall tree.

Sameer tried to explain his thoughts. He said, "By flat, I mean the situation is so single-coloured. It's like everything is looking white. I do not want to discount the solution to Mr. Mohan's problem. That was extraordinary, Aryakt. And I think only *you* would have done it. A person who is so disciplined in his thoughts. An artist can realise an art."

Madhava interrupted, "Only an artist can realise an art."

Sameer nodded.

"You were destined to solve Mr. Mohan's problem, Aryakt. So, you did it. Who would have thought that a person like you.... Pardon me. But considering your anxiety about being with people, one cannot imagine you coming this far. From Vizag to Kerala. Am I right?"

Aryakt nodded understandingly.

"Say something, Maddy," Sameer said aloud.

"I am trying to see this bird here, but it isn't visible clearly. It's a peculiar bird. I didn't see any of this kind anytime."

"Not a surprise, Maddy. There are more than, I think, ten thousand species of birds."

Madhava looked at Sameer appreciably and said, "Wow. I think you got this information during your career as an Ornithologist. Isn't it?"

Sameer realised Madhava was teasing him. He said as a counter-satire, "Yes, of course. It was during the same time when you owned a multi-national software company."

Both the friends laughed aloud.

"I am destined to solve the problem of Mr. Mohan and Mr. Gnanavel. I agree", said Aryakt and continued:

"But with what had happened in Vizag, I am destined to solve *my* problem as well. Remember, both are mysteries—Mr. Mohan's problem and now, my problem. I recollect instances that led me to take this up. An elderly stranger helped me when I was lost on the outskirts of Vizag. You guys trying to make me come out of this anxiety and get me to the party. Sheela Aunty - how is she related to me? Why should she try so much and help me get out of my anxious behaviour?"

Aryakt's following sentence surprised the friends. He said, "I know, Madhava, you were behind the scenes. You requested

Sheela Aunty to make me talk and perform in front of the guests. Isn't it?"

Madhava felt astonished. *How could he know this?* He nodded in silence.

Aryakt said, "Every instance that occurred was willing to motivate me to get out of this behaviour. As you said, Sameer, I should be destined to take some risks now. I am destined to think. I never did anything in my life so far that isn't my cup of tea. But life has thrown a challenge at me. I should accept it. I accepted it."

Aryakt got up from the ground and started walking around. He continued, "I get motivated from the takeaways. I try to look into the intent rather than the actual statement. And vice versa at times. And only that had helped me understand Mr. Mohan's problem and solve that mystery. Now, Sameer's words have triggered another important thing for me."

Aryakt's eyes looked bright. He said, "Sameer said that everything is looking single-coloured and white. My friends, what is the white colour? Isn't it the mixture of various colours? I should individually realise those colours."

The friends looked at him in surprise. Aryakt continued, "Madhava, can you go to the tree and see if the bird is still there?"

Without any cross question, Madhava went to the tree, looked towards one of the branches, and moved his head.

Aryakt then asked, "Are you able to see it?"

"No," Madhava answered.

"If Sameer had not diverted your attention, what would you have done to fulfil your eagerness to see that bird?"

Madhava then moved to the other side of the tree and looked at the beautiful multi-coloured bird visible clearly.

Aryakt then said, "Isn't it visible now?"

Madhava nodded.

Aryakt smiled and continued, "The same thing I should do now. Look at the important things from another angle."

Sameer's eyes narrowed. He asked, "Which important things?"

"The photograph," Aryakt said.

❑

Chapter 31

After reading Mr. Mohan's novel, Aryakt realised that the story revolves around a place named Vatakara. Google suggests that the place is along the coastline and has lovely beaches.

"Isn't it possible that the beach in the photograph is one of those beaches in Vatakara?" Aryakt said, looking at the copyright page of the novel. It read the release year as 1999.

As the two friends thought about it, Aryakt continued, "It is quite likely. The novel was released in 1999. The photograph also should have been captured during the same time. Given Mr. Mohan's state of mind after all these years, imagine the situation after he had just released his novel on Amita."

Madhava said, "Do you think Mr. Mohan could have forced his two other friends to visit Vatakara, and that's where this photo was clicked?"

"There you are. Exactly. Isn't it possible?"

"Certainly possible," said Sameer.

"It means......" Madhava abruptly stopped and continued after a moment as Aryakt and Sameer looked at his concerned expression.

"It means the secret that the photograph holds has some strong connection to Amita."

Sameer raised his eyebrows and said, "What is so special about this girl, man? Even after thirty-odd years, she is making her presence felt."

"She *was* special, according to what Mr. Mohan had written in his novel."

"What's the novel about? Can it throw some light on our problem?" asked Sameer as he felt a gist of detective inside him.

"I don't think so. But we can visit Amita's home in Vatakara, but we are unsure if her family is staying at the same place," said Aryakt, and Madhava immediately said,

"You Aryakt. You are initiating a visit to some unknown place, to some unknown house, and talking to some unknown people. That is quite unbelievable." Madhava said, looking at Sameer.

"That's what. Unbelievable this is. Aren't you afraid of people anymore?" Sameer asked.

"I am. You see, my forehead. It started sweating again. My heart started to beat faster again. But it's inevitable for me. My comfort is urging me to stop right here. But my desperation is motivating me to go ahead."

"That is what we wanted to see in you, my friend!" said Madhava.

"Thanks to the desperation," continued Sameer.

"We are here. We are here," said Madhava, holding Aryakt and wiping the sweat off his forehead.

"Let us first get the address of Amita's residence from Mr. Gnanavel," Madhava said, smiling and trying to comfort Aryakt's panic.

"*Chalo* Vatakara" said Sameer aloud.

As the rental car raced towards Vatakara, near Perambra, Aryakt started observing the photograph keenly. It was sunset time; the friends were smiling happily. The background has quite a few coconut trees growing on a small mountain. The date printed on the back of the photograph read Dec 8. The year wasn't visible clearly.

There was something written on the sand that wasn't understandable either. *It should be the sunset for sure, not the sunrise. Anyway, it can be made sure once we visit the Vatakara beach*, Aryakt thought to himself and announced:

"Let us go to the beaches first. It is already 4 PM now. It would be the sunset time. What say?"

"So, Amita's house during the night? It sounds scary," Sameer said with a half-smile.

The car driver helped the friends to get to various beaches. The only thing they observed was the background. They would get down and analyse if it matched somewhat with the photograph. Some beaches didn't have any mountain (which was present in the picture) nearby. Some didn't have a similar view. Discarding the obvious ones, the friends reached a beach, and its background looked like the photograph's.

The friends got out of the car in a hurry. The beach was relatively silent, with not many people around. Only a family with two kids was seated at a distance. The beach was quite neat and peaceful.

"It looks almost similar, Aryakt. See those coconut trees. The mountain terrain has some differences, but there are people now on the mountain, too. There are some small houses there." Sameer said.

"It is quite possible. Isn't it? Thirty-odd years are sufficient for a beach to transform. And as the constructions happen, the terrain should change slightly as we try to view it from quite some distance," Madhava explained.

All the while, Aryakt just observed the beauty of the place. He felt the infinite water saying something. As he brought himself to the current situation again, the friends decided to take a photograph standing similarly, at a similar angle and with a similar view of the background. The other family on the beach helped them take the photo.

The excitement wasn't controllable for the friends. They jumped onto the iPhone of Madhava to see and compare the characteristics of it with that secretive, mysterious, and treasure-holding photograph.

"Almost the same buddy. There are some differences, yes. But those ought to be there. Look at the place of sunset. Exactly the same. This is the beach. Yes, this *is* the same beach." Madhava said.

"We found it, Aryakt. We found it." Sameer said, laughing as the other family seated at some distance felt surprised about what was so fascinating about the photo they clicked.

Aryakt couldn't believe the moment. It was the happiest moment in around two months for him. The fog surrounding his thoughts was getting cleared. The beach almost looked the same.

Since the beach was found, the friends started to inquire about the surroundings, holding the photograph in their hands. There was a turtle museum at some distance from the beach. Hopefully, and with excitement, the friends asked if someone knew anyone from that photograph. No one could recognise anyone.

The friends approached the nearby houses and asked the residents, especially the older people. No one could recognise the three old men in the photograph.

"There is something written on the sand. Can you figure out what it is?" Aryakt asked Madhava and Sameer.

They observed it keenly, but they couldn't figure it out.

"Shame on us," said Sameer.

"I can send the capture of this photo to one of my friends. He is an image-processing expert. He'll have tools to magnify the image and figure that out." Madhava said.

"Please do it." Aryakt requested.

After sending the picture to Madhava's friend, they went to the nearby restaurant for dinner.

"We should party. It is a big achievement, friends. We have found the beach on which the photo was clicked around thirty-two years back. I am sure the secret lies in Amita's home. We are quite near to solving the mystery now, Aryakt. Hold your breath." Sameer said excitingly.

The words *hold your breath* made Aryakt lose some breath. Multiple possibilities popped inside his head, and the jumping thoughts never stopped. As they got out of the restaurant, Aryakt said in his panic voice,

"I am afraid now. I don't know if I want the secret to be cracked and face what lies on the other side of it."

"What!?" exclaimed Madhava.

"Yes, Madhava. I am afraid. We don't know what's waiting for us in Amita's home. What if they accuse us of something? What if the friends in the photo have committed a big crime? What if Amita's family has been waiting for us all these years? And what if....." Aryakt stopped abruptly.

Madhava and Sameer were in shock listening to Aryakt. Aryakt then continued his sentence.

"The tagline of the novel was *What if she was here!* And now, I ask the same thing. What if she was here? Right here, with us. Watching us."

❑

Chapter 32

The friends wanted to laugh aloud genuinely, but they couldn't. However, they tried their best to laugh at Aryakt's comment. From inside, they shivered a little. All these years, Mr. Mohan's delusion wasn't just his imagination. It seemed real to the friends in some aspect, at least.

As they approached the address provided by Mr. Gnanavel, the friends stayed silent. Aryakt was thinking something profound. His intense glare at nothing was intensifying the already built-up mysterious aura. The autorickshaw stopped at the correct address, and it was around 8 PM. The street had little light illumination since there were only two streetlights far apart.

They saw a light bulb glowing on the veranda as they approached the entrance gate. Sameer feared it to be a haunted house as he could feel the thick darkness along the street. Aryakt suddenly stopped at the entrance gate and requested his friends follow him. He then walked along the street, crossing the house. A big tree was on their right, and a newly painted metal chair was empty.

"The ending scene in the novel is right here, where Mr. Mohan sees the ghost of Amita seated on this metal chair. Maybe that left him astonished for the rest of his life." Aryakt said.

Sameer coughed aloud multiple times, and the friends realised that he was shivering with fear.

Madhava held himself in control and said, "Don't correlate the instances of that novel with real life. Mr. Mohan was a fiction writer. He has created things. So, he might have imagined things."

Aryakt suddenly jumped across as if someone had pulled him and sat on that metal chair. In the darkness of the night, the friends couldn't see each other's faces. The big, dense tree has masked the hardly available light illumination. As the friends saw a dark figure on the chair speak out, they wanted to believe that, indeed, Aryakt spoke.

"Something is wrong for sure. I was thinking all the while after the dinner. Yes, something is completely wrong. I wasn't sure till this time. But now I know what's wrong. *This* is not the beach we are after. This definitely is not the beach."

The friends were surprised and shocked at Aryakt's behaviour.

"What are you talking Aryakt? We are here to talk to Amita's family and try to understand if they have any knowledge about the photograph. Nothing else. So, what's wrong here? And how are you so sure it is not the beach we are after? It looks almost the same. And as we thought, time changes the geographical terrains slightly."

"No, it is not the beach we are looking for. I can prove it." Aryakt said as the friends looked at the dark figure on the metal chair.

"Prove it? How?" asked Madhava. Sameer stood silently and wanted to leave the premises at any cost. He was ready to pay anything to witness the morning sun immediately. Darkness in the street with Amita's residence beside them and the current circumstances made him shiver.

"Give me your phone," Aryakt asked, and Madhava gave him his latest iPhone.

"Please put on the flashlight," Aryakt asked.

Madhava did so.

Aryakt was searching for the photograph in his bag, and unknowingly, he had focused the light beam on his face. Sameer jumped in shock for a moment, looking at Aryakt's face. "He is Aryakt, don't worry. Even *you* look like a monster with the light illumination in that angle." Madhava said, observing Sameer. Aryakt then focused the flashlight on the photograph and explained,

"This evening, we have tried our best to click the photo at an alignment similar to the alignment of this photo. Isn't it?" Aryakt said and continued as the friends nodded. "Okay then. So, the picture we clicked looked almost the same as this mysterious photograph, though the people were different. Am I right?"

Madhava nodded.

"And that is the whole problem. It looked almost similar. But my understanding says it shouldn't be." Aryakt said with confidence that was unusual and surprising to the friends.

"Shouldn't be similar. What's your point, Aryakt? Where are you getting to?" Sameer finally spoke as he saw his excitement of finding the mysterious beach fail.

"I am coming to that. Listen to me carefully. This mysterious photograph was clicked on December 8th, and the year is not so clear in this. It could be somewhere in the year 2000 to make it believable. Do you agree?"

The friends nodded thoughtfully.

"And this is our photo that was clicked today," Aryakt said as he showed the new photograph.

"Now compare both," Aryakt said, placing both the photographs side by side. Since the mysterious photograph was not visible in the darkness, Sameer took his phone and focused its flashlight on it.

"They look similar, Aryakt. And you say that's the problem. Now tell, why?" Madhava asked.

"Look at the Sun. The sunset position is the same. It might not be the same, but it is certainly similar. Am I right?"

"Yes. So what? That's what we need."

"No. That's not what we need. This photograph was clicked in December. We are now in June. The sunset pivot point moves towards the southwest every month. The sunset point must be at a different place on the photograph *if* clicked on this beach. It should have been somewhere near these coconut trees. Geographical terrain may change. But not the sunset pattern. Having the sunset at a similar place in June and December proves it is not the beach where the photo was clicked."

Sameer turned the focus of his flashlight on Aryakt's face to make sure he, indeed, was Aryakt who was talking. It was Aryakt with his eyes glowing brightly. He then shifted the focus onto Madhava's face. A confused expression showed up. Following the pattern, he then turned the flashlight on his face.

"Why are you doing it, Sameer?" asked Aryakt.

Sameer cleared his throat and said in a cinematic way, "Well. Okay. It seems I am the only one who is confused here. Isn't it? Everything is so clear. Am I right, Maddy? This pivot point and all. Damn, clear."

"I am...... I am fine. I am doing good." Madhava replied strangely.

"Yes, there you are. No one asked you if you were fine. And your answer proves that you are confused too," Sameer said, and

Aryakt understood the need of the hour. He then held Madhava's hand, and the three of them got under the nearest streetlight, which was a little far from Amita's residence.

"See friends. I know it is a little confusing, but believe me, this is not the beach we are searching for. Let me know if your image processing expert friend comes back with what those characters on the sand are." Aryakt said.

Madhava and Sameer looked at each other. Sameer murmured, looking at Madhava, "Back-to-back bouncers," Madhava smiled in response.

Preparing themselves mentally before entering Amita's residence wasn't a big task for Madhava and Sameer five minutes ago. There was just a glitch of suspicion. But the last five minutes have changed the perspective of the present scenario. They didn't know what they would say to Amita's family. As it was clear (at least Aryakt was quite confident about it) that the beach under interest was not the one they visited during the evening, there was no point in the friends talking to Amita's family. After analysing the situation, Sameer said:

"No point in getting in. Why should we talk to Amita's family now? What's the motive?"

Madhava pushed his teeth, piercing his lower lip, and thought for a while. He then said, "That's..... That's correct. Why do we go in now? Seeing the uninvited guests will be a shock to the family. Frankly, I cannot initiate any discussion with them."

"Me too. Let's go from here." Said Sameer.

They looked at Aryakt for his approval. He stood silent for a moment with closed eyes. He took a few deep breaths and said, "I'll initiate the point. You be beside me, silent. Is that okay?"

Madhava coughed, clearing his throat. Sameer laughed.

"Are you saying that you'll initiate the discussion? In this situation, with an unknown family, at the residence of a girl whose ghost is supposed to be seated on that metal chair where you were seated just five minutes back. Do you remember you did discover Amita's face on the wall? Don't you think the ghost, if, must choose someone from the three of us, will choose you?"

"Could be. But I lived so afraid of people that ghosts don't bother me. Ghosts aren't dangerous, but humans, at times, are," Aryakt replied and walked towards the gate.

The two friends were surprised to see Aryakt with such confidence in thought and with such force in his body language. They followed him, acknowledging his gutful move, and felt quite happy to see their friend being confident, coming out of his anxious behaviour.

The beach isn't the one that we are looking for. The mystery is still open. The secret still needs to be unveiled. Am I missing any clue? No, I didn't. Madhava and Sameer are missing their important professional schedule. What was the text on the sand? Will I know what it is? Will it have any connection to the secret? How will I understand that connection?

Aryakt's thoughts were realising the bitter truth that it was the wrong beach they visited. The surroundings started spinning. It seemed to him that some force was stopping him from entering Amita's house. As the small entrance gate creaked open, Aryakt lost the grip of his hand on the gate and fell on it, leaning his upper body on the gate. Madhava ran forward and held Aryakt.

"Oh no. What happened? Let's go from here, Madhava. This is not the place to stay anymore. I am sure Amita's ghost doesn't want Aryakt to get in her house."

Madhava looked at Sameer in shock.

"Yes, I believe that. Let us go away from here." Sameer replied in confidence.

The friends took Aryakt towards the main road, holding his hands on their shoulders. Aryakt was half awake, but he felt the surroundings spinning continuously. Physically, he was getting away from Amita's residence, but his mind and thoughts revolved around the home. He felt the cool breeze in that street touching his skin like a sprinkle of water on a drying leaf.

Aryakt never oppressed his thoughts. Being gentle with his thoughts was comfortable for him. But his good, in fact, excellent friends were cruel to his thoughts presently. His physical self needed some rest. He tried to look back at the residence as the friends struggled to get him to the main road. But he gave up as turning back would restore his decaying excitement to meet Amita's family.

Is Amita from somewhere around here calling out my name? It seems so. Aryakt thought, and while being in a wholly surrendered mode, he closed his eyes.

❑

Chapter 33

Let Me Fly!

"The remote isn't working well. I should press each key so hard for the TV to detect it. Go and call the manager." Sameer asked Madhava as the early morning sun rays made their way into the room through the opened windows.

"Hello. You, too, can go and call the manager. Going downstairs doesn't need any Visa stamping." Madhava replied in irritation.

Sameer raised his eyes and murmured, "Well. Okay. I'll check if the TV buttons work properly."

Aryakt opened his eyes and heard Sameer murmuring. He tried to lift himself, but it was hard for him. He rested his whole body on the right elbow, pushing hard, and lifted himself to sit.

"How are you feeling now?" Sameer asked as he stopped changing the channels at the Discovery HD.

Aryakt's voice sounded tired at first, but his intent wasn't. He said, "I am okay. Did you get any reply from your image processing expert?"

Madhava smiled as he realised Aryakt was in his good form again. He replied, "I didn't touch my phone. Need to check if he has replied," he said and checked his phone.

Aryakt got up from the bed and looked at Madhava curiously. Madhava checked the notifications and read the message from his friend.

"Hey, Maddy. It is the number '24' on the sand. I say this with 95% confidence, and the tool used to check it is 90% reliable. Make your corresponding calculations as to whether or not you believe it. By the way, the uncles in the photo are having fun."

"Is he working in any MNC?" asked Sameer.

"He was. Currently, he is doing freelancing for some good start-ups." Madhava replied.

"Thought so. Terms like confidence and reliability used with corresponding percentages are standard MNC styles. Good to know." Sameer said.

"Is he sure about it, Madhava?" Aryakt asked, ignoring Sameer's statement.

"Definitely. My friend may sound funny, but he is a tech gem. It should be the number '24,'" replied Madhava as he was ready for Aryakt's response as to what to do next.

There was a knock on the door. "It should be the food delivery guy," said Sameer.

Sameer opened the door, and Aryakt brushed his teeth while thinking something deep. After around ten minutes, Sameer opened the breakfast-packed boxes. It was *idli* all the way. Madhava sounded disappointed, looking at the sight. Aryakt was indifferent.

"Didn't you find anything else, Sameer?" Madhava asked with an irritated face.

"It is healthy, Babu Moshay."

"I can't eat it early morning," Madhava said.

"Can't you eat *idli*? Wow. See there. Bear Grylls is having a rotten cockroach as his breakfast." Sameer increased the TV volume.

"No. No. I'll eat the *idli*. But after breakfast, let us find a source of flowing water and walk along it to reach some human population along with Bear Grylls."

The friends laughed aloud happily as the nostalgia of *Man Vs Wild* got to their minds.

"Before you start anything, listen to me once. Sameer thinks Amita's ghost doesn't want you to enter the residence. It may look ridiculous, but that wasn't the case last night. There is something around that house. I cannot assure what, but there is some energy around that house." Madhava said as Sameer looked at him agreeably.

Aryakt smiled, looking at his friends. He didn't have much energy to explain as his mind was entirely occupied by the number '24'. Sameer continued the discussion.

"What happened to you actually at the entrance gate?"

Aryakt thoughtfully said, "It was just giddiness due to overthinking. We were at various beaches all day, you know."

"These days have been hard on you. And we can see a tremendous change in you, Aryakt." Sameer said.

"A change that's for the good," Madhava said, smiling.

"Close the window, please, Sameer," Aryakt said, continuing as Sameer closed the window and switched on the fan.

Aryakt signalled the friends to focus on the matter. He said in a low voice as if he was cautious of keeping the words within the room.

"The number '24' should have a definite connection with the secret we seek. But we need to be sure of one thing: Is that marking on the sand a temporary one made before clicking that photo? We must make sure of it. Can your friend send us the cleaned-up photograph, Madhava?"

Madhava smiled heartfully and said, "He did send me the cleaned-up photo along with the explanation of '24'. Here it is."

Aryakt looked at Madhava, smiling. Zooming at the text on the sand, Aryakt could now vaguely make out the text '24'. It was better than the original photograph. It was deliberately written on the sand.

Aryakt swallowed. He then looked at Mr. Srivatsa in the photograph and thought: *How can I not think of you as my grandfather? You were the one who gave me my name. You got me admitted into the orphanage. I know why. You had to serve the nation through the army. And then... And then... something unexpected happened. You met with an accident. You never knew that you'd not be awake for the next twenty-two years. And now, here I am, realising that you are not my grandfather. You are smiling in this photo. A great smile. A sweet smile. But what thoughts were those bright eyes hiding behind them? What plan do you have? If I am not your grandchild, then why am I here in the scenario? Who am I after all? If you are to trick someone, then why did you choose me? Didn't you realise that my emotional conscience is at stake? I was always under the impression that I had a blood relative around me, even though you were in a coma. It brought some energy. But now, I am left alone. Why did you do this to me? Your smile makes me angry and brings tears to my eyes simultaneously. But let me try. I can't hold my emotions away from you. The connection I never had so intense with you is now getting there. I don't know why. Let me swallow the uncertainty.*

"Tell me one thing. Why are we behind the secret now? Mr. Srivatsa is not your grandfather. What's the point in going ahead on this?" asked Sameer.

Madhava said before Aryakt could answer Sameer, "I am confused."

"I'll have to take it up because I am destined to solve this mystery, and probably some treasure is waiting for me on the other side. No emotions are linked as it is proved that Mr. Srivatsa isn't my grandfather." Aryakt lied.

"Whoa! That's so straightforward from you, man." Madhava said, laughing.

The three friends slept for some time as the previous night was tiresome. Aryakt was awake, looking at the rotating fan and thinking. The whole circumstance might have got on top of Sameer's mind. He spoke in his sleep. He murmured, "Why leave a clue hidden in the photograph? Instead, one should have avoided giving a clue."

Aryakt heard it, smiled, and looked at the rotating fan again. After a few minutes, he, at once, recollected what Sameer murmured in his sleep. That triggered a striking thought in his mind. He thought *that if the clue in the photograph was deliberately given, it was for me to understand. Otherwise, what's the point of providing that clue? So, if that clue is deliberate, then it means that Mr. Srivatsa wants me to solve the mystery. When the clue is here, its associated pathway to the solution should also be. But where?*

Aryakt woke up, tearing multiple white papers from his notes; he started sticking them on the wall using glue. In another fifteen minutes, there was a big whiteboard on the wall. Aryakt started writing various probabilities on it. The pivot clue is the number '24'. But something needed to be more convincing. If anything convinced him of being the pathway, it didn't direct him in any way.

As Aryakt continuously murmured to himself, Madhava woke up from sleep. As he started talking to Aryakt, Sameer woke up irritated. Aryakt felt sorry for his friends. Their help was becoming overwhelming for him. They were accompanying Aryakt, ignoring their busy professional schedule. But it was inevitable for Aryakt to keep thinking and get somewhere.

Madhava and Sameer got up from the bed and read all the possibilities on the newly made paper whiteboard.

The friends got together yet again to discuss the possibilities and their probabilities of being true. Suddenly, Aryakt recollected an empty small bag among one of Mr. Srivatsa's belongings. He took that out from his bag and started examining it.

"That's the empty bag. I saw it yesterday." Madhava said.

Aryakt kept the empty bag aside, and the friends started discussing again. As Aryakt moved around the room talking, he observed that there was something that was glittering inside the open bag. He rushed towards it and examined it. There was a thin circular button stitched in the interior of the bag. Also, there were some stitched lines around it. The same stitched lines were on the opposite side of the interior.

"What's this?" Aryakt asked aloud.

The friends looked at the bag and closely examined it. "Looks like some locally stitched design. Bags like these are available," Sameer said ignorantly.

"Yes, Aryakt. There's nothing magical here. We do get various patterns of designs on the bags these days. So, it should have also been there back during those times." Madhava said.

Aryakt looked at the circle keenly, touched the stitch linings, and moved his finger along the lining interior of the bag as he cautiously traced its shape. After around a couple of minutes, he got up from the chair and asked:

"You are right. The design on the bag isn't anything new. But think once, guys. These kinds of designs are mostly on the top side of the bag. Obviously, for their beautiful looks. But did you ever see any bag whose interior is designed like this?"

Silence for a moment. Then Sameer answered, "No."

"Yes. There is no point in having any beautiful and patterned design interior to a bag where the exterior looks plain."

"Let us pull the interior out and see what that design comes up to," Madhava said excitedly.

Aryakt smiled, sat on the chair, and said, "I know what it is."

"What? And how do you know without looking at it completely?"

"I have run my fingers through those stitched linings, and that shape has to be the world map."

Madhava's eyes got narrowed. Sameer said, "World map?"

"Yes. It must be the world map. Let us cut the bag and open it out."

The friends then carefully cut the bag using a knife and opened it completely. As Aryakt turned it upside down, a world map clearly showed up, with the circular button precisely in the middle of the map. Madhava and Sameer were astonished.

"There you are. It's a world map. And I am sure there should be a link between the number '24' and this map."

Madhava and Sameer were still transitioning, and it was hard for them to believe Aryakt's words. After a few minutes, Madhava was in this world again and asked, "What is that circular thing there? Is it the centre of the map?"

Aryakt said, "Yes. Seems so."

Sameer said something quite interesting out of nowhere. He said, "Is that circular mark where the secret beach is?"

Madhava felt overwhelmed by Sameer's guess and patted his shoulders. The friends looked at the circular button's placement and realised it was somewhere in the Atlantic Ocean.

"Oh no," Sameer said.

"Isn't the centre of the earth a landscape? Is it the ocean?" asked Madhava.

Aryakt thoughtfully replied, "It depends on the cartographer. Or the person who drew this map. But the thing to focus on is that the circular button almost feels like it is at the centre, and that is an Ocean. Not even close to any beach."

Another hour went by, discussing various other possibilities. But nothing looked concrete. Aryakt always thought there should be a link between the number '24' and the map.

Does it mention 24 hours, indicating that the beach is 24 hours off-timed to India? In that case, why one needs a map?

Does it specify the date on which the photograph was clicked? Is that date on the back a lie again?

Is this assumption of linking the world map and the number '24' correct at all? The world map looks quite evident since it was deliberately designed on the bag. But is the number '24' a coincidence? Someone else might have written it, and unexpectedly, it was captured in the photograph. But no. Everything is placed with utmost detail. It shouldn't be a coincidence. These old men aren't foolish or ignorant. Everything in this photograph is deliberately crafted and then captured.

Aryakt, at once, got a thought. "Please be here. I'll be back in a moment. He left the room and returned with a protractor in five minutes."

The friends realised his guess and smiled. Sameer said, "There you are. The soldier with his deadly weapon."

Aryakt smiled, neatly placed the map on the bed, and drew a line through the circular button, representing the 'so-called' equator. He then put the protractor, aligning its base to the equator and its centre to the circular button. Placing two marks at 24 degrees towards the left and right, he said:

"If we draw two lines from this circular button till these two points, certain sections of the world will fall on those lines. The same analysis would apply to the mirror images of those lines on the other side of the map."

Sameer just looked at him with an open mouth. Madhava hesitantly asked, his heart beating fast, "And then?"

Aryakt exhaled profoundly and replied, "And then, we need to find the beaches that fall on those lines by googling about those places."

The friends sat on the chairs and exhaled. It wasn't a relief for them but a preparation for what was coming next.

For another couple of hours, they searched various beaches and found that at least twelve beaches fell on the two lines in quite the opposite parts of the world.

"This is a world tour, my friend. Nothing less than that," said Sameer, and Madhava just nodded. After some time, Madhava said, "It is ridiculous. It's such a humongous task. And what if we don't find any beach that resembles it? And even if we find one, what would we do with the beach? Do we claim that beach as *our* property?"

Aryakt had no answer for it. He just remained silent. But he was thinking something.

It shouldn't be this. I must have mistaken something. How can one be so detailed and so stupid? Aryakt thought as he walked onto the terrace, signalling his friends to stay in the room.

He got onto the terrace and felt restless. *Twelve beaches! What a shame!* His frustration was showing up in the form of anger. Aryakt being frustrated was a rare occasion. Being angry to such an extent was almost impossible. He couldn't believe himself being in such a phase where he was angry with someone. The biggest surprise was that he was angry with himself for being unable to correctly predict, assess, and analyse the clues.

His frustration peaked as he moved faster around the terrace railing, hitting his fist against the fence with good force. An acute pain started in him. He held his right hand with his left and regretted his action immediately. When he turned around the palm and looked at it, the skin was scratched, and there were blood marks on all the finger joints. The sand finish of the terrace made the impact worse. Every minute, the sand balls created multi-folded pain. He removed all the sand from the finger joints with utmost care and gentleness.

The pain gave him the feeling of losing his grandfather. Even though it's a lie now, there was still a person who was supposed to be his grandfather. Two big tears scrolled down his cheeks. *Why can't it be true? Tricking someone to this extent is horrendous. Everything was just a trick. Just a lie. All these years were just a lie.*

Touching the hard and dry sand with his fingers, Aryakt's mind floated in the air to catch one of his thoughts. It flew along with the words he murmured. In all the words of 'lie'' there was a hidden truth. He tried to catch his thoughts by recollecting what he said just a minute back. Truth had struck like lightning. The unbearable pain was losing its impact. The truth was taking the charge. He thanked the floating air, the terrace, the railing, the sand, and most importantly, he thanked his frustration.

Aryakt ran down the stairs, taking three steps at a time. He almost fumbled at the room door.

"Open! Open!" he shouted.

Sameer opened the door at once and was surprised, looking at Aryakt. Aryakt pushed him away and rushed into the room. He hurriedly opened his bag and took the photograph out. He opened the windows and took the photograph towards the sunlight. Observing it keenly, he looked disappointed.

"Give me the cleaned-up photograph, Madhava" he asked. Madhava opened the photograph in his phone and gave it to Aryakt as he observed the blood coming out of Aryakt's finger joints.

"What happened to your hand?" asked Madhava, and Sameer bent down to look at it.

Aryakt ignored the question and keenly observed the photograph, zooming in on its needed areas. Aryakt's expression changed drastically. He then handed over the phone to Madhava and jumped on the bed. He slept, looking at the rotating fan.

"I should have observed it at first. It would have saved me from this wound," Aryakt said, looking at the surprised friends.

"Firstly, can you tell us what happened to your hands?" Sameer asked.

"You guys care about me a lot. I just hit the railing with my fist out of frustration."

Madhava raised his eyebrows, looking at Sameer.

"And now, let me tell you what I found out. It was all in front of us, all the time."

"What was in front of us?" Sameer asked, confused.

"Mr. Srivatsa tricked me by lying about some specific things and building his narrative. Keep this in mind and look at his index finger in the photograph."

Madhava and Sameer zoomed in on the photo and keenly observed Mr. Srivatsa's index finger.

"Yes, there is something on his index finger. Can't say what it is," Madhava said, still confused.

Sameer doubtfully said, "I think it is the sand. Isn't it?"

"Yes. It is," Aryakt shouted.

"So?" Madhava asked.

Aryakt laughed aloud and said, "Think. Think."

After a couple of minutes of thinking, both friends shouted at once that they understood the point. Sameer overtook Madhava's voice and said,

"Mr. Srivatsa wrote the number '24' on the sand."

Madhava continued, "So the text '24' is a lie."

Madhava and Sameer fell silent suddenly.

Madhava said in dismay, "What does that mean?"

Aryakt observed the disappointment on his friend's face and said, "Don't worry. We know that Mr. Srivatsa manipulates his words and tricks people, and so do Mr. Srivatsa know that *we* know about it. So, the number 24 should now be reversed. So, it becomes 42."

After becoming convinced of Aryakt's theory, the friends started searching for the beaches along the lines at 42 degrees from the circular button along the equator. And to their extreme surprise, only one beach was on the two lines.

The Rovaniemi beach in Finland.

The friends were in tremendous shock after realising there was only one beach, which the photograph had been pointing out for all these years.

"I can't believe it. How deeply was this secret immersed in." Madhava said in surprise as his eyes were filling with tears.

"How did you think of all this Aryakt? You are a genius, man." Sameer said, looking at Madhava, expecting a sentence from him.

Madhava understood it and murmured it in Sameer's ears. He said, "Records have broken."

Sameer and Madhava hugged, realising that Aryakt wasn't the same person anymore. Both asked at once.

"So, should we go to Finland now?"

Sameer took his phone and started checking how far Finland is from Switzerland.

Aryakt stayed silent for a moment and said, "You guys have done more than any friend could have done for his friend. Let me take it alone. Let me fly."

❑

Chapter 34

Tiesin Sinun Tulevan

The white envelope was quite big, and it was evident to Aryakt by its weight that it contained more than one piece of paper. A lady came into the room with Aryakt's permission and offered him a coffee. Aryakt didn't respond as his senses tried to take in the happenings. She pleasantly asked another very neatly dressed office boy to keep the coffee pot on the table. The tray that held the coffee pot was astonishingly decorated.

Aryakt looked around the room, and it was beautiful. There were pictures of various great authors and their books. The treatment that Aryakt was getting made him overwhelmed, and he just sat silent for another five minutes. He drank some water from the glass beside the coffee tray. He then held the envelope in his hands and opened it carefully. There were four papers in it, handwritten. The papers weren't regular. They were heavy and brownish. They looked authentic.

He looked at the first page of it. The handwriting was almost perfect. The heading read 'Tiesin sinun tulevan'. He then read the other content of the page randomly to see if the same unknown language persists. But no, it was all in English. He started reading the text, unaware of what was about to come. The text read:

I knew you would come. I knew you would come, Aryakt. But I don't know how old you are now. Maybe in your twenties. I can only imagine how you look because you are sleeping now on the bed beside my writing table. I am sure you look like your father, or your mother, or your aunty, or maybe like me. Haha. Never mind. I know you'll be a good man. Do you want to see yourself with me? Then, recheck the envelope. You'll find a photograph.

Aryakt moved his hand into the envelope and found a photograph. Mr. Satyavratha was smiling heartfully, looking at the baby sleeping on a bed. His heart melted, understanding that Mr. Satyavratha, whom he didn't focus on at any time, was probably his grandfather. And the way he smiled at the baby, which was Aryakt himself, made his eyes full of tears. He wiped them off and replaced the photograph in the envelope. He continued reading.

Now, it's not the time to cry, my boy. Wipe out your tears. I can understand the challenges that you have faced to get here. But believe me, it'll be worth it. Tiesin sinun tulevan. Don't be confused. It's Finnish. It means 'I knew you would come'.

Aryakt closed his eyes, and tears fell on the paper. He moved the paper away and continued crying. Someone so confident about a person like Aryakt wasn't a thing that he ever imagined. He was a born loser. People didn't care about him. People made fun of him. Exhaling out all the negativity, he continued reading.

Be a Roman in Rome – Do you know this phrase? I say, be an Indian in India. Since you are reading it in Finland, shouldn't you read at least the heading in Finnish?

Let me start with this. Weren't you an introvert all your life, Aryakt? Weren't you scared of people? Afraid to talk to people. I was like that during my childhood. I shivered, looking at people.

I stammered while talking to them. I enjoyed being alone. My mother and father tried to help me, but I never helped myself. I realised it after they left this world. Being an introvert is not a sin. But ruining your life because of it is indeed a sin. I realised it too late. My parents couldn't see me confident throughout their lives. Even now, I owe them a big sorry. Anyway, I married Saraswathi, your grandmother, and had two children. Saraswathi left me alone after she had some complex disease of nerves. I adjusted myself to be happy with my kids, Ramakrishna (your father) and Surekha (your aunt).

Ramakrishna was a genius in academics. Surekha was blessed with musical talent. People used to flow with her voice whenever she sang a classical song. Everyone said that the kids were Saraswathi putras. I never felt wrong about those people for leaving me away (and using my wife's name alone) from that credit. Just kidding. I was proud of them. But, as they grew, the introvert behaviour increased multifold. They stopped talking to people. Ramakrishna, at first, hesitated to go to school, but later he ultimately refused. Surekha stopped singing even in front of her friends. Her friends distanced from her due to her behaviour. Ramakrishna lost his confidence. Even the relatives made fun of them at times. Initially, they were good and helpful. But as time progressed, the relatives felt it necessary to keep their kids away from Ramakrishna and Surekha.

I and Saraswathi tried to help our kids a lot, but we couldn't. We needed a doctor's help, but there wasn't much access to proficient Psychiatric doctors. Anyway, the available doctors couldn't help them. Even the college life didn't help them. The social anxiety increased with every day. Ramakrishna used to teach kids at our home since kids never made him feel anxious. Surekha practiced music at home. We thought marriage would fix this issue, but it didn't. Surekha married a businessman, and her behaviour made her curse herself. She knew she wasn't making her husband happy. She always stayed at home.

Ramakrishna got married to a great lady, Vishalakshi (your mother). She had a patience like the mother earth. With her presence, Ramakrishna felt confident.

Tears flowed down his cheeks as Aryakt heard his mother's name, and he didn't bother wiping them out. The moment deserved it. He looked around the room and continued crying, imagining his mother and father.

But Vishalakshi lost her life in a road accident, and that had left Ramakrishna breaking into pieces. Within the next 6months, his anxious behaviour and loneliness made him commit Suicide. Just imagine Suicide! I was left alone. The phase that made me happy during childhood made me despair when I got older. The world seemed empty. Whom should I blame for the loss? I hate the word anxiety while being in anxious mode. I was almost about to commit Suicide, but I heard your voice cry. The cry had a message for me. It's a message for people like me—an urge to save a child.

Aryakt shivered. He could see the paper in his hands move as his hands were shivering.

No, Aryakt. Do not let the anxiety get over you. Calm down, please. I know it's heart-breaking to listen to these things, but you should keep yourself strong now.

You were around one year old when both your parents died. And they died of what? The introvertism and extreme social anxiety. I had it myself. Doctors said that it can be hereditary. It was almost likely that you'd inherit the intelligence but also the introvertism. I shivered at once. It was then a plan was born in my mind. What does it take to come out of introvertism? Help. Yes, it is a small help which could last a lifetime. If not the parents, who would help a child come out of such extreme heredity? My answer to it was 'none'.

As I have been researching a lot on this problem since childhood, I knew that adversities can potentially bring a person out of this phase. I didn't want you to lose yourself to this anxiety. The mindset is always the cause. Working on it could only get you out of it. I am getting older now, and given the cardiac problem, I don't know how long my life will last. So, I planned something for you.

There are two very good friends of mine: Mohan and Srivatsa. Mohan is a bright author. He is pretty healthy and may live for many years. Srivatsa is an army person. He has rock-solid health. All the three of us planned for an excursion. I explained everything and my plan, too. We got to Finland, the place you are right now. The understanding was to lay a path to a treasure that should belong to you. Do not expect much here, my boy. I am not rich.

There could be no one who can take care of you after I am gone. There are relatives, but they might not do it for long. Given the high chances of you being an extremely introverted person, it is unlikely that the relatives might help you for long. Being a burden for someone is as bad as being anxious about talking to people. With a heavy heart, I have decided to admit you to an orphanage in our native place, Visakhapatnam. The place is close to my heart, and Vizag will prove good for you.

Aryakt took a deep breath and recollected the air of Vizag. He felt desperate for it for a moment.

I have asked Srivatsa to get you admitted to the orphanage in Vizag. I am very sorry for doing it, my boy. I want you to be confident. Who else can give you enough confidence other than the world itself? Insults are inevitable. I want you to go through that path and emerge victorious. To accomplish it, there should be a challenge for you. Srivatsa will be coming to you once in a year. If health permits, I'd love to come and meet you. He'll be observing your mindset and any characteristics of introvertism. He'll certainly help you in case you build any such thing. Once you are grown up, he'll explain to you about this challenge of finding the treasure. You'll see a peculiarity with Srivatsa. He is........ No, I'll not disclose it. That's the part of the plan. If you are reading this, you have realised it very well. Yes, he tricks people in a great manner. It is his way of teaching. I am unsure what he told you, but I know it took your efforts to crack it down. If you are lost in between this challenge, Srivatsa will help you.

Directing you to Mohan first is my wish. I want you to know about him. About his accomplishments. You'll get to know about it for sure. That aura will stay with him for a long time.

You may still be confused about why I did all this. Let me clarify. The world will never forgive a person who cannot help himself. Remember that. And don't get to the conclusion that the world is cruel. No. It isn't. It is full of people like you and me. Who is scared of something. Who loves something. Who wants to avoid something. Who wish to accomplish something. Everyone has their problems, my boy. Everyone. It would have been an arduous journey from childhood for you all these years. But we'll have to realise it's been a tough journey for everyone. The people around us are like us. Just like us. Love them. If you are angry with someone, be angry. No issues. But at the end of the day, remember, they are like us. The love between two persons is what is keeping this world alive.

The orphanage, the teachers, the friends should have been your world for all the while. But as you have now come this far, don't you feel you are no longer introverted? Aren't you realising you have broken the barriers you set back in your childhood? Aren't you wishing to talk to people now instead of running away or escaping them? Isn't the world looking a bit more compassionate? If your answer is 'yes,' then my plan is successful. This journey of finding the treasure and especially solving the mystery should have given you a need to get yourself out of the most comfortable and restricted phase of life – 'Being alone.'

I hope you have some friends. At least 'two' should be so close to you that they should have helped you solve the mystery. However, I am unsure of it. But I wish you to have two such lovely friends. Good friends. Great friends.

Aryakt held his tears inside him and continued reading.

Srivatsa would have explained the photograph and visit to Mohan to you, and he would have given you the proper clues with the correct emphasis that you are challenged to your limit and come out victorious at the same time.

I am not so old, but I am old now, Aryakt. Aryakt is the name I chose for you. I hope you like it. I have this cardiac problem, which I don't want to name. But I might not live long now. I believe in Srivatsa. He'll take care of you. If he is doing good, then convey my thanks to him. And I believe in you, Aryakt. Thanks for making my mission accomplished. Now, the world is yours.

Wait! I know you are not behind that treasure anymore. But it's my responsibility to let you know about that. All my life, as I struggled to make my parents feel confident about me, regret is what pinches me all the time. As a person who has seen a lot happening due to introvertism, I feel responsible and eligible to write something for the people around there and let them know that the world is like us, after all. So, I have written quite some books on it, around twenty. I don't know if people would like to read my writing. But they are enjoying it so far. Have you come across any of my books? Your father used to read a lot. Anyway, I write with a pen name of aNoNyMoUs. I'll be glad if you've come across any book, but if not, then try reading one. I don't want to enforce my passion on you. Read it only if you want to.

Aryakt blinked his eyes continuously, trying to take in the fact that his favourite author, aNoNyMoUs, was his actual grandfather. He realised why he always felt that his books exactly spoke about the issues he faced daily.

Now, coming to the treasure that Srivatsa told you.

The copyrights of all my books are with me right now. But my lawyer would transfer it to your name after my death. A reasonable sum of money should be in your account if the sales are good. I believe my publisher. They are genuine. But, as I said, I wonder if people will continue reading my books. But that's what I can give to you, my boy.

And finally, I hope you live a life full of confidence, happiness, and courteousness toward fellow human beings. I'll sign off now. I can understand your pain now as I say goodbye to you. Your grandfather isn't with you in person. But my thoughts are always around you and reflect in my books.

"If you can do something good, then the biggest crime you can commit is not doing that good. Life is all about knowing and doing 'that' good which you can do."

Happy journey back to India.

❑

Chapter 35

A Question That Still Exists

The circumstance was beyond belief. Aryakt found himself in threshold consciousness as he touched the letter with his fingers and realised the wish of an old man. *Is this happening in reality? Am I in this library, or am I still in Vizag and dreaming?* The lady knocked on the closed door, and Aryakt didn't know how to respond. He stood up and said, "Please come in."

As she came in and walked towards Aryakt with a pleasant smile, Aryakt recollected his grandfather's words: *They are all like us*. The words echoed in his mind. He realised that he hadn't been in his comfort zone for the last few weeks, but that wasn't the bad phase of his life. Not at all. He had met people, spoken to them, helped them, understood them, and realised that people out there were having their problems that they were dealing with, with utmost sincerity.

He thanked his grandfather for such a fantastic plan to turn him into a social personality (not that that was needed to survive, but that definitely was required to look towards the world from a different perspective). He wasn't afraid of the lady. Instead, he smiled back and brought his right hand forward for a handshake. They shook hands, and the lady requested Aryakt to wait for some time as the library association president was on his way to meet Aryakt.

Leaving apart the effect of knowing that the library association president was coming to meet him, Aryakt felt that the impact of the present moment was more significant. Aryakt touched his forehead with his left hand and surprisingly observed that it wasn't sweating even after shaking hands with an unknown lady in a foreign country without any known person around. Aryakt looked at the letter and smiled. He thought, *my grandfather did what he had to do. Now it's my turn.*

After around fifteen minutes, two persons entered the hall. The first person was a tall, fair, middle-aged man who looked dignified. The second person was a short, brown, and royal-looking old man.

"Hello, young man. I am Lucas Salonen. I am the president of the association of this library. And this is Mr. Vallabh Rao, your advocate."

As they took the two chairs across the table, Mr. Lucas said, "Let me clarify why I say Mr. Vallabha Rao as your advocate. He is the advocate of Mr. Satyavratha, your grandfather."

Aryakt nodded thoughtfully.

Mr. Lucas continued, "I hope you have read your grandfather's note. His words are private to you and him, and none of us know what lies there. The instruction to every president of this library was the same. That was to hand over Mr. Satyavratha's note to his grandson. And that will be the one with a particular photograph we have a copy of. And now, here you are with the same photograph. I wonder how time brings things and people together. This instruction was such a mystery for everyone who has been in this position. There were previously six people in this position, and to be frank with you, I feel lucky to have witnessed this mystery being solved. I wish you all the very best. I hope we have successfully protected the note and accomplished our responsibility of handing it over safely to you, the righteous owner of it. I'll hand over the further proceedings to Mr. Vallabha Rao, who has been a very loyal advocate of your grandfather."

"Okay. Thank you, sir." Aryakt replied in confidence.

Mr. Lucas left the hall, and Aryakt was left with his advocate in the hall.

"How are you, Aryakt?" Mr. Vallabha Rao asked the right question for the moment.

"I am good, sir," Aryakt replied, which was a surprisingly significant accomplishment. Aryakt wished that Madhava and Sameer were seated beside him right then. But he recollected the words in his grandfather's note - *Everyone is like us*. Then, he looked at Mr. Vallabha Rao and smiled heartfully.

"How do you feel reading your grandfather's note? Are you happy with it?" the advocate asked.

Aryakt was surprised with the question. He tried to figure out how to answer it and said, "Well, I believe I just have been successful in what my grandfather wanted me to do, sir."

"Wow. That is a great thing to hear. I truly wish your grandfather's soul would be ecstatic now. He was a great man. I had known him just one month before he left Finland and later, I got the news that he died out of the cardiac problem. He believed me, Aryakt. Just realise his trust in people. I cannot believe that I am releasing this burden off my shoulders. I'll not question any of the content of that note, but I wish and am quite certain that it has a good impact on you."

Aryakt's eyes filled with tears. The advocate moved forward and kept his hand on Aryakt's shoulders. As Aryakt looked at him, the advocate said, "You look like your grandfather. I remember tears in his eyes when I saw him for the last time before he left Finland. Thanks for coming this far, Aryakt."

"No, Sir. It was my responsibility and probably my destiny to come here."

Taking out some documents from his black leather bag, Mr. Vallabha Rao said, "Let me come to the actual point. The responsibility that your grandfather had given to me. *You* will be the sole nominee for all of Mr. Satyavratha's assets. And here are the three assets: number one, the two stored building in Helsinki. Number two is the total remaining cash in his bank account, also accounting for the interest for all these years as per the bank's norms (I made the tax payments of the cash for all the years which will be deducted from the total sum). Number three is the copyrights of his twenty books and the royalty of those books for the previous thirty-five years. I have been working with the publisher every year, and the royalty is credited to the account in which the remaining cash is being held. His books are best sellers in all the countries they released."

Mr. Vallabha Rao started taking some papers from his bag as Aryakt was just seated silently. The next thing that the advocate said left Aryakt in total astonishment.

"So, leaving apart the settlement of the two stored building (for which the maintenance and repair charges are to be negated), the total cash, which also includes the royalty of twenty books for thirty-five years minus the income tax, is approximately 9.4 million euros. And this accounts for approximately eighty-five crores Indian rupees."

The route to Rovaniemi Beach was quite beautiful. Aryakt's request to visit the beach during the sunset on the same day was sincerely fulfilled by Mr. Vallabh Rao. He sent his Mercedes along with his driver to pick up Aryakt. The driver was quite friendly, and talking to him made Aryakt feel good. Aryakt remained silent most of the time during the travel.

"The sun should be there for around fifteen minutes now, sir. Do you want your picture clicked?" asked the driver, Basheer.

Aryakt didn't feel any interest in a picture. There was no thought in his mind to capture the sunset. The day brought him so many surprises that he didn't feel any need to catch the sight around him. The words of his grandfather were echoing inside him.

"No," he replied plainly and sat on the sand, looking at the sunset.

There was no one around on the beach. A beautiful beach being empty during the sunset was quite surprising to Aryakt. He, however, felt nice to be alone. The driver stood near the car, away from the beach. The emptiness was almost fearful, but Aryakt was on the edge of being happy, alone, and terrified as no one was around. The loneliness in an unknown country started disturbing his senses, and he breathed heavily.

Aryakt never felt an urge to clear his vision. His eyesight was always perfect. But the present moment brought some blurry view. He rubbed his eyes twice to interpret what was before him correctly.

Madhava and Sameer walked towards Aryakt in doubt. As they neared him, they ran toward him laughing. Aryakt unknowingly started laughing. The sunset now looked beautiful to him. There were many people around enjoying the sunset. The people whom he never spoke to. Never looked at. But the very people around, whom he was afraid to talk to or even look at, were there for him now, making his breath restore to its original pace. *Was I imagining that I was alone on this beach? Is my anxiety telling me a goodbye portraying itself for the one last time?*

Madhava and Sameer still ran towards him, but his state of mind worked faster than ever. Aryakt realised the beauty of the sunset. He realised the very sunset was terrifying for him a minute before, but now it's beautiful. The only change was in his vision of realising that people were around. The people around made the sight beautiful. He realised that the people around you can make things more beautiful. This time, he didn't complain about being anxious all the time. Instead, he realised that the people around him were just like him.

Aryakt got up and ran towards his friends. As they touched each other's hands, Aryakt felt a sigh of relief. Tears automatically emerged from his eyes. But this time, it was not because the friends were his saviours. Instead, it was because their presence made the environment more pleasant. To his friends' surprise, Aryakt said aloud:

"How great to see you here, my friends. You are here at the right time."

Sameer instantly replied, looking around the crowd, "Yes, yes. We know why."

"No. No. You don't," Aryakt replied, smiling as he waved at the driver and signalled him to bring his camera.

"Who is that?" Madhava asked in surprise.

"He is Basheer. My new friend." Aryakt said, smiling.

"Friend?" Madhava and Sameer asked at once.

Aryakt started running towards Basheer, who had an advanced DSLR camera in his hands. Aryakt took it from him, and Basheer got back near his car again.

"Let us click a picture. Let's go to that place." Aryakt said and moved towards the less crowded place. The friends just followed him.

"This is the correct angle. The sunset, the bent coconut tree, and three friends in the picture. Isn't it?" Aryakt said as he winked.

"Wwwhat?!" Madhava laughed.

Aryakt moved across to a girl and asked, "Can you please take a picture of us?"

"Sure," the girl lifted her goggles to her head and took the camera.

Aryakt asked Madhava and Sameer to join him as he stood in the middle. The girl was trying to focus the camera on the three friends, and Aryakt suddenly said, "Wait, please."

He went across and wrote something on the sand, and rushed back. He then asked the girl, "Can you please take our picture along with the text on that sand, sun, and that bent coconut tree on the mountain?"

"Perfect," replied the girl.

A wind ran over the three friends as Aryakt set his beautiful hair right. The scene looked picture-perfect with the smile on Aryakt's face and the surprise on Madhava and Sameer's faces.

"Ready, one, two, click," the girl said, smiling.

"Thanks a lot. I am Aryakt from India."

"Okay. I am Leena." She replied.

"Thanks again," Aryakt said, and the girl joined her friends.

Sameer, with narrowed eyes and opened mouth, looked at Aryakt. He couldn't control his words anymore. He asked, "What's going on here? Are you.... Are you Aryakt? What did you write on the sand there? And first of all, tell me how you dared to talk to that girl?"

The flight took off from Helsinki to Mumbai, and the friends adjusted themselves in their seats. After around one hour, Sameer recollected the question he missed to get an answer. He asked, looking at Aryakt, who was seated between him and Madhava.

"By the way, what did you write on the sand before we took the photo? I couldn't see it because the water wiped it off. It isn't quite clearly visible in the photograph too."

"Contact the image processing expert." Aryakt said and winked.

"It was a roller coaster ride. Isn't it?" said Madhava as they got off the flight at Vizag airport.

"Yes, it was," said Sameer lazily as he felt sleepy.

Madhava then asked, looking at Aryakt, "What do you make of it?"

"Nothing much," Aryakt said as he was thinking something.

"He should be thinking of the money now," Sameer replied.

No answer came from Aryakt. Madhava then asked Aryakt as they got into the cab, "What are you thinking, man? It's a new life now. You are not the same Aryakt who left Vizag some weeks back."

"I have two questions on top of my mind. First, how much zeal would it take to get over the effect of the coma and convey the information about the secret? How could Mr. Srivatsa accomplish it? It's beyond my imagination."

"And the second?" Sameer asked.

"I would like to meet the person who painted Amita's picture on the wall. How can I find him? He might have left some clues regarding himself in that painting. Every artist has their signature style. Isn't it? I am sure that his signature is hiding somewhere in the painting. I should have noticed it. I am afraid that Mr. Gnanavel will get that wall repainted. I should go to Kerala soon."

The friends sat silently as the rental car moved towards Aryakt's home. The happenings of the last three weeks had a significant impact on their thought process. Seeing Aryakt change so much made them happy. Sameer looked at Madhava and smiled. Madhava responded with a half-smile.

"He isn't our innocent Aryakt anymore." They exchanged the words through their eyes.

Madhava informed Mugdha about their arrival to Vizag, and as the friends reached Aryakt's home to drop him off, Mugdha and the other tuition kids welcomed them. All the kids surrounded Aryakt and hugged him in ecstasy.

"We missed you," Vilohith said, crying.

Aryakt touched Vilohith's hair and smiled. He then said, "I am here again."

Mugdha approached Aryakt and said silently, "I am done with the advanced Trigonometry chapter."

Aryakt nodded.

The kids forced Madhava and Sameer to get into the home.

"I'll stay here for a while. You people, please get in," Aryakt said.

Aryakt sat on the metal chair on the footpath and started thinking. After around fifteen minutes, Madhava, Sameer, Mugdha, and the other kids got near the terrace railing and saw Aryakt seated on the chair, thinking deeply.

After around a minute, the sea breeze of Vishakhapatnam overlapped the surroundings. Aryakt moved his head up at once to set his hair right, looking against the direction of the breeze.

Everyone looked at Aryakt with surprise since his eyes weren't fearful anymore. They were full of confidence but tired for the moment. Aryakt looked up and saw the group looking at him and smiling. He smiled back.

The kids shouted, "HERO."

Aryakt thought about the big question now on top of his mind: *Why did the friends choose Finland?*

❑

Chapter 36

And Then...

Around a couple of weeks later, Aryakt started packing his stuff as he was moving to another penthouse near his current house. The majority of his luggage was 'books'. He planned to pack the kitchen luggage last.

This luggage doesn't need a trolley. But what if it rains? Better to book a proper and protected trolley. The monsoon was still in a week. *Kerela should have already kissed the monsoon breeze*, he thought.

The void all through Aryakt's life wasn't there now. He wished to go out to meet his friends. The friends with whom he lost touch after schooling. He wanted to meet every one of them.

As Aryakt started arranging the luggage, he lifted the old heavy mattress on the only cot. There were some greeting cards that his students gifted him on his birthday and on teacher's day. He packed them carefully. The reflection of the tube light fell on his eyes from another corner of the cot. He looked at that side and was surprised at the oversized plastic raincoat. The 'so-called' raincoat.

Aryakt took it at once and ran his hand through it. The incident with the old man flashed in his mind, and he realised that that person was the reason why Aryakt took up the challenge of cracking the mystery behind the photograph.

Locking the penthouse, carrying the raincoat, he took an auto-rickshaw to the outskirts of Vizag, where he met the old man. He exited the auto-rickshaw and stood beside the highway, trying to find the big tree. As he could locate the tree, he ran towards it and hoped to see the old man. No one was around. *How stupid of me*, he thought.

He then started looking at nearby places but couldn't see anyone. Getting under the tree again, he sat peacefully. Scratching the bark of the tree, he was lost in some thoughts.

He looked up at once. A small polythene cover was hanging from a branch and leaning on the stem. He got up, held the cover, and looked inside it. There were some bread pieces. He untied the cover from the stem and found a paper in it with handwritten text. Reading which Aryakt got his heart in his mouth.

It's not over yet. Finland wasn't the only destination. The hunt would begin at Chamoli.

This time, don't forget to bring the ***original*** *Aryakt.*

❑